# "You thought I was going to make a pass at you."

There was amusement in Clay's voice.

"No," she said again. "Of course not, I know you wouldn't...." She stopped. He thought she would have objected, whereas on the contrary...

"You know nothing of the kind." There was a kind of anger in his voice now. "You know nothing about me." He was only a foot away. "What would you do, Jenni, I wonder, if I did kiss you?"

Now that it seemed likely to happen, she was afraid. She had a feeling that once she'd been kissed by Clay there would be no going back.

"I...I have to know someone very well, be sure that I like them, before I enjoy being kissed."

"You always do it that way around?" he asked. "Why not try living dangerously for once?"

**ANNABEL MURRAY** has pursued many hobbies. She helped found an arts group in Liverpool, England, where she lives with her husband and two daughters. She loves drama: she appeared in many stage productions and went on to write an award-winning historical play. She uses all her experiences—holidays being no exception—to flesh out her characters' backgrounds and create believable settings for her romance novels.

## Books by Annabel Murray

### HARLEQUIN PRESENTS
933—LAND OF THUNDER
972—FANTASY WOMAN
1029—NO STRINGS ATTACHED
1076—GIFT BEYOND PRICE
1148—A PROMISE KEPT
1188—A QUESTION OF LOVE
1228—DON'T ASK WHY
1259—BLACK LION OF SKIAPELOS
1283—ISLAND TURMOIL

### HARLEQUIN ROMANCE
2549—ROOTS OF HEAVEN
2558—KEEGAN'S KINGDOM
2596—THE CHRYSANTHEMUM AND THE SWORD
2612—VILLA OF VENGEANCE
2625—DEAR GREEN ISLE
2717—THE COTSWOLD LION
2782—THE PLUMED SERPENT
2819—WILD FOR TO HOLD
2843—RING OF CLADDAGH
2932—HEART'S TREASURE
2952—COLOUR THE SKY RED

# ANNABEL MURRAY

## let fate decide

## *Harlequin Books*

TORONTO • NEW YORK • LONDON
AMSTERDAM • PARIS • SYDNEY • HAMBURG
STOCKHOLM • ATHENS • TOKYO • MILAN

For Judy and Phil
my 'antique' friends

Harlequin Presents first edition February 1991
ISBN 0-373-11340-4

Original hardcover edition published in 1989
by Mills & Boon Limited

LET FATE DECIDE

# CHAPTER ONE

'JENNI! Jenni!' Sonia Crawford hissed, nudging her cousin. 'Look at that man over there, the way he's staring at you.'

It was her laugh that had first attracted Clay Cunningham's attention. Musical and uninhibited with an appealing catch in it, it rang out above the noisy buzz of the market place and made him curious to see its owner, to discover if her appearance was as appealing. After all, it did no harm just to satisfy his curiosity, he excused himself at this deviation from his self-imposed rules. With an eagerness he had not known in some time —an eagerness that should have bade him beware —he had threaded his way through the meandering throng of shoppers, until, standing as he did head and shoulders above everyone else, he had a clear view of the stall and the two young women behind it. He had no doubt which one of them it was that had laughed, luring him here siren-like.

His first thought was how tall she was. Gracefully tall with a proud upright carriage. Unlike many tall women, she did not seek, by stooping, to conceal her height. And the laugh had not misled him. She *was* worth looking at. But what was it about her exactly, the indefinable something that stirred him in a way he had not experienced for some time?

Until recent years—and the circumstances which had made him put a tight rein on such appreciation—

7

Clay had always considered himself to be something of a connoisseur where attractive women were concerned. And generally he had always been able to sum up in a few apt phrases just where their attraction for him lay. But this young woman baffled description—at first. He found himself edging casually closer. For just a while longer he would allow himself the forbidden indulgence.

Yes, his intent scrutiny told him, she was far from the accepted design for beauty. No simpering chocolate-box lovely, this. There was too much irregularity of feature. Nor did she fall into any of the other categories he recognised or that had ever before appealed to him—way back when. He stood arms folded, legs firmly planted, as the shopping crowd surged around him, ineffectual waves against his rock-like immobility.

Hers was an entirely original face, he decided, with its subtly merging planes. She had a wide, intelligent brow, smooth cheeks, their olive skin healthily tinted with rose—a colour which he would swear owed nothing to a cosmetic palette. Her mouth was generously large like everything else about her. Was it possible, he wondered with the cynicism of a man often disappointed, that she had a generous nature to match? She had a stubborn jawline that spoke of determination, but of integrity too. There *were* women of integrity in this world. A pity those who'd touched his life had been of the other kind.

It was a strong face altogether, he thought. His attention, first caught by a whim of curiosity, was now firmly held. He found himself wanting her to laugh again so that he could see her mirth light up that grave, serene face. And—the almost urgent need caught him by surprise—he would like to be the one to induce that mirth.

'*Excuse me*, young man!' The tetchy sound of irritation from an elderly lady tugging an overladen shopping-trolley made him realise how long he had been obstructing the flow of pedestrians. He apologised profusely, charming the complainant with his good looks and his sincerity. Then, mingling with other browsers surrounding the young woman's stall, he began to inspect her wares. They were like those on a hundred other so-called antique stalls. Jugs of various shapes and sizes, plates, books, postcard albums, other people's unwanted junk. Nothing in his line to warrant such interest. And yet still he lingered, from time to time taking a surreptitious glance at the stallholder, adding to his inventory of her appearance.

She was looking enquiringly at him now and he realised she had become aware of his scrutiny. Her lips parted in the smile he had been waiting for, revealing white teeth, perfect but for one slightly crooked tooth which should have marred her appearance but somehow didn't. He found himself returning her smile.

'Can I help you?' she asked. Her voice was a lovely dark husky instrument, and now that he was closer he could see that her eyes were grey. Great soft-grey eyes, widely spaced, their expression as serene as her features. He found himself thinking wistfully that a woman with eyes like that might deal frankly and honestly with a man. Her hair defied adequate description. The nearest he could come to it was a mahogany red, satin-smooth, drawn back off her face into a loose knot. He could imagine how, released from its confinement, it would tumble about her shoulders, a rich, glowing veil. He found himself picturing those shoulders,naked, as soft to the touch as her hair

would be. A convulsive shudder ran through him.
And, annoyed with himself, he snapped out of the
imaginings into which he had strayed. It was a long
time since he had allowed himself to dwell on such
eroticism. He ought to move on, be about his
business.

'Can I help you?' she said again, a puzzled note in
her voice.

If only you *could* help me, he thought. Quite at
random he picked up a trifle from the stall and asked
the price, trying—somewhat belatedly—to give the
impression that his stare had merely been intended to
catch her attention.

She told him the price, then turned to another
customer. Clay stared at her profile, half obscured by
the upturned collar of her expensive-looking winter
coat. She was better dressed than the average
stallholder. In fact, altogether, there was something
about her that made her surroundings incongruous.
He felt unreasonably piqued. Once upon a time,
having gained a woman's notice, he had been
accustomed to holding it longer than that. Without
undue vanity he had been aware, nevertheless, that
he appealed to women.

It had been some while, of course, since he had
consciously tried to gain and hold a woman's notice,
so he was surprised to find himself wanting to arouse
this girl's interest and retain it. But that was
madness, a self-indulgence he couldn't afford. Just as
well she seemed indifferent. With a little grimace of
self-mockery he shrugged and moved on.

'Wow! That was some hunk of man!' Sonia, whose
totally contrasting appearance had not drawn a
second glance from Clay, nudged her cousin again.
There was a note of humorous envy in her voice as

she went on, 'What a dish! And he was certainly giving *you* the once over!'

Jenni laughed. It was the same full-throated, joyful sound that had first drawn her to Clay's notice.

'That's putting it mildly, Sonia,' she told her much younger companion. 'The way he was staring, I was beginning to think I was supposed to know him. Wish I did,' she added wistfully. 'I like tall men.' She wished too that their conversation could have been prolonged instead of being restricted to a mere question and answer. But something about him had made her feel oddly shy. She had turned her attention to another customer to hide her confusion and, when the sale had been made, the man was gone.

'Wasn't he tall?' Sonia drooled.

It wasn't often she encountered a man tall enough to look up to, Jenni thought. But this one must have been well over six feet. Broad-shouldered too, and muscular. Healthily tanned for this time of year. He had looked the outdoor type. A wealthy playboy, fresh from the winter ski-slopes? Somehow she didn't think so. She'd met many of that sort, and he hadn't been well enough dressed, for one thing. A local farmer perhaps, or merely the owner of a sun-bed.

Her study of him hadn't been as overt as his of her but, despite a certain embarrassment at the intensity of his scrutiny, she had gained an overall impression of a man she would dearly like to know more about. Just for the sake of satisfying her curiosity? No, she admitted with characteristic honesty, there was more to it than that. There had been a sudden sharp thrust of attraction.

However, she sighed, she didn't suppose their

paths would cross again. They certainly hadn't before. She would have remembered. Then an enquiry from a prospective customer broke across her train of thought. Albeit somewhat reluctantly, she put the tall man out of her mind and returned to more business-like considerations.

'Well, that was a good day's trading!' said Sonia as she and Jenni packed the left-overs into their van.

Ormskirk market day was always a busy one but perhaps because of the unseasonably good weather people had been in a better-than-usual buying mood. For January it had been almost springlike.

'Mmm. It's a good thing there are some auctions coming up soon.' Jenni clambered into the driving-seat. 'I'll need to replenish our stocks.'

Sonia was pessimistic.

'If the "out-of-town mob" don't outbid you.'

Though it was illegal, it was still known for some dealers to gang up in 'rings' in order to keep others out of the bidding for some valuable pieces. Jenni had been approached more than once by a representative of such a confederacy but she had steadfastly refused to join in their machinations.

'I'd rather deal honestly or not at all,' she always told her cousin.

'I might take a trip down to London the week after next,' she said as carefully she negotiated the one-way streets. 'That's where all the quality stuff is. And you can even find the occasional bargain in the city markets—*when* the stallholders aren't the sort that use Sothebys and Christies price lists as their bedtime reading!'

'I wonder what sort of day Auntie Phyl's had in the shop,' said Sonia as they drove home across the flat almost featureless countryside—farmland mostly, with the only landmark a towering gasometer.

The market stall was not the girls' only trade outlet. Together they ran Jenni's shop, Serendipity, a small but prosperous side-street property just off nearby Southport's Lord Street. Phyllida Wallis who helped out on market days was really Jenni's great-aunt and no blood relation to Sonia. But the cousins both referred to her affectionately as 'Auntie'.

'Let's hope she's had a busy day too,' said Jenni. 'She hates having nothing to do.'

You needed patience to deal in antiques, Jenni always thought. It could be tedious when business was quiet. Fortunately trade at Serendipity was nearly always brisk. Though the sea had receded a long way from Southport this had in no way interfered with the town's popularity as a resort, and visitors came from all over the country, for as well as its miles of sand and distant glimpses of the Welsh mountains Southport's famous Lord Street offered splendid facilities for shopping.

'Tell Auntie about your latest conquest,' Sonia prompted Jenni over high tea that evening. On market days, once the shop was closed and the day's accounts done, no one had the energy to cook an elaborate meal.

'What's this then, Jenni dear?' Phyllida Wallis asked eagerly as Jenni blushed. A spinster herself, a fact she deplored, Phyllida longed to see her great-niece happily married. And the fact that Jenni had reached the age of twenty-five without any serious long-term involvement troubled the older woman.

'You shouldn't listen to Sonia's rubbish,' Jenni told her aunt. She felt a little uncomfortable about her moment of violent attraction to a complete stranger.

She sought to make light of the matter. 'She's talking about some man who probably thinks he's God's gift to women. He was eyeing us up, that's all.' But despite this disclaimer she had a feeling—almost of pain—that she was doing the stranger an injustice.

'Eyeing *you* up, you mean,' Sonia retorted without rancour. 'I wouldn't have minded him looking at *me* like that—as if he was totally gob-smacked. And if he had you can bet I'd have found some way of getting to know him.' She proceeded with great enthusiasm to give Phyllida a catalogue of the stranger's attributes. 'A craggy sort of face, but not ugly. Very bright blue eyes that seemed to look right through you.'

Remembering the effect those eyes had had on *her*, Jenni could not repress a shiver of pure sensuousness.

'How old?' demanded Phyllida.

Phyl was as bad as Sonia, Jenni thought, listening in rueful amusement to their exchanges. And yet there was a vicarious pleasure in hearing the attractive stranger described.

'Hard to tell.' Sonia was judicious. 'He had a lot of thick fair hair. The springy sort you'd like to get your hands into. But it had a lot of grey in it. Late thirties I'd say, wouldn't you, Jen?'

'I didn't take as much notice as you obviously did,' said Jenni mendaciously, because she *had* noticed quite a lot. And for her the man's most riveting feature had been his long, firm mouth. The narrow upper lip had spoken of an impatient nature. But the lower lip! Its fullness had hinted at passion. She quivered inwardly again.

'It's about time Jenni had a serious boyfriend,' Sonia declared roundly, for all the world, Jenni thought a trifle indignantly, as if she were discussing her cousin in her absence. She had had boyfriends, of course and she had grown very fond of one or two of them. A couple of them had proposed marriage but she had never met anyone with whom she could imagine herself spending the rest of her life. Because for her marriage was for keeps.

What kind of man *was* her ideal? she wondered idly, and instantly the thought was rewarded by a mental picture of the tall stranger. For heaven's sake! she adjured herself.

'Have you see this man around before?' Phyllida Wallis was asking, and again it was Sonia who answered.

'No! If we had we'd have remembered, wouldn't we, Jen?' And Jenni had to agree. 'But in future, I for one shall be looking out for him,' Sonia said.

Jenni made no further comment. But two days later, at the Saturday market, she found her eyes constantly straying over the heads of the milling crowd, searching for a tall, powerful figure, for a head crowned with greying blond hair. And she was aware of strong disappointment when he didn't show up.

It was ridiculous. And yet Jenni couldn't pretend that it was only because Sonia had made such a thing of it that, in the days that followed, she couldn't get the tall stranger out of her mind. Unlike Sonia, she had no confidence that they would ever see him again. It was probably one of those cases of 'ships that pass in the night'—a casual visitor to the area. But though she had made light of Sonia's comments, to herself Jenni couldn't deny that the man *had* seemed unduly interested in her.

She was accustomed to arousing men's interest.

But, being essentially modest, she couldn't imagine
what they saw in her. A lot of them tried to engage
her in flirtatious conversation. They seemed to think
being a market stallholder made her fair game—an
error into which those she served in the shop never
fell. Jenni didn't care to be a casual pick-up. And yet
if the tall man had attempted to get into conversation
she had a feeling she would have reacted differently.

'Fancy coming to the sale with me tomorrow?' Jenni
asked her cousin on the following Tuesday
afternoon. She had just come back from viewing the
various lots and there was an air of barely suppressed
excitement about her that prompted Sonia to ask,
    'Good stuff, is it?'
    'There are some excellent pieces of porcelain. But
that's not all. You know I've been looking out for
some good paintings for that man in Liverpool? Well,
I think I've found just the thing.'
    'In our local sale-room?' Sonia was incredulous.
    'I'm not sure anyone's realised what they are.
They've come from a house clearance and they're just
listed in the catalogue as 'four small oil paintings' and
they're covered in dirt. I didn't dare pay them too
much attention in case some of the other dealers
noticed. But, Sonia . . .' and she lowered her voice as
if even here someone might be listening, 'I've got a
hunch. I'm sure they're rather special. If I can get
hold of them at a reasonable price it'll mean a hefty
profit.'
    'Surely the big picture dealers will be after them?'
    'They might not be there.' Jenni was still tense with
excitement. 'They only come when there are a lot of
paintings for sale and these are the only ones. The
emphasis is more on furniture. So, would you like to

come? It's about time you gained some experience of the sale-room.'

'I'd love to. But what about the shop?'

'I'll ask Auntie if she'll do an extra day.'

There was no problem getting Phyllida Wallis to stand in for Sonia and the two girls arrived at the sale-rooms in plenty of time to get a good position under the auctioneer's rostrum, where it would be easy to catch his eye. The large room was already filling up with would-be buyers.

'Some of the big boys *are* here.' Jenni had spotted a group of prosperous-looking men chatting, as if idly, on the far side of the room. But she knew their conversation would be anything but idle. 'But they're mostly furniture dealers, as I expected. Unscrupulous Ursula's here too,' she discovered. 'That definitely means there'll be a ring.'

The ring's method was for its members not to bid against each other, thus keeping prices down. Afterwards the cartel would hold a second 'knock-out' auction among themselves. Ursula Bond was one of Jenni's principal rivals at auctions and often occupied a stall next to the two girls.

'Ursula's not the only person here we know!' Sonia exclaimed. 'Look who she's talking to!'

The amorphous knot of men had shifted, hiding some of their number, bringing others into prominence, and Jenni stiffened as she saw the face Sonia had already recognised.

'It's your admirer,' Sonia said, and Jenni was aware of a strong feeling of disappointment. Surely he was not of the ring's unprincipled number?

As if her gaze had carried some telepathic message, the tall man turned in her direction and over the heads of the milling viewers their eyes met and locked. Jenni had the electrifying sensation of something linking, tightening between them. Then one of his companions said something, touching his arm, and the thread of communication was snapped.

'Bet you he tries to chat you up today,' said Sonia.

'If he's one of Ursula's cronies I'm not sure I want him to.' But throughout the morning, as the sale progressed, Jenni found her gaze wandering again and again in the tall man's direction. And on a couple of occasions she actually found him staring fixedly at her. On the second of these occasions she took herself to task. He would be getting the wrong impression soon, thinking she was trying to pick him up. And for the rest of the morning she concentrated fiercely on the auctioneer's homely features.

It was customary for the auctioneer to break for an hour for lunch. Though some of the dealers brought sandwiches, others adjourned to a convenient nearby public house. The two girls could have gone back to the flat. But, 'Come on, let's go to the pub,' Sonia urged. 'I bet tall, bronzed and handsome does. He's bound to, not being a local.'

By the time they entered the public house both bars were crowded but they managed to squeeze themselves into a corner, at a small round table.

'I'll order,' Sonia said. 'What are you having?'

There was quite a queue at the bar for drinks and pub grub and Jenni resigned herself to a long wait, passing the time in one of her favourite occupations—watching people.

'OK if I sit here?'

Jenni's heart skipped a beat. A familiar tall figure was hovering at her table, a glass in one hand and a loaded plate in the other. He obviously didn't expect a refusal, for he was already sliding on to the bench seat beside her, leaving the only chair unoccupied.

'You're at the sale,' he said unnecessarily. 'Bought anything yet?'

'One or two small pieces.' Jenni's heart was pounding now and she felt oddly breathless.

'Me too. I get quite a kick out of auctions,' he said, 'don't you? Beating down the opposition.' Then, 'I'd better introduce myself.'

Why, she wondered with a faint quiver of nerves. Was it just a courtesy or was it, in Sonia's words, that he'd decided to chat her up?

'Clay Cunningham,' he volunteered and looked expectantly at her.

'Jenni. Jenni Wallis.'

'Hello, Jenni.' He held out a large, long-fingered hand and after a split second of hesitation she put her fingers into his.

She had always hated limp, wet handshakes and long ago she had made sure her own was firm and decisive. But she didn't think she had ever been on the receiving end of a handshake like Clay Cunningham's. Strong and warm, it was an extremely pleasant experience, and when he did not immediately release her hand she began to be aware of strange sensations. A tingling that seemed to begin with her fingers and travelled up her arm, ending in strange secondary sensations in other parts of her body, and she felt oddly bereft when he finally released her hand. But he seemed satisfied and began to eat his ploughman's lunch, his strong white teeth taking large chunks from the crusty bread roll.

Watching him, Jenni wondered about him. His shirt, sweater and trousers were immaculately clean and pressed but certainly not new or expensive-looking. He didn't exude the air of prosperity that somehow would have fitted his striking appearance.

'Penny for your thoughts,' he said suddenly, catching her off guard, and startled into a frank reply she told him.

'I was wondering what you do.'

Fortunately he didn't seem put out by either her frankness or her curiosity.

'My partner and I deal in antiques—mostly furniture. Precarious way of earning a living, isn't it? Fluctuating trade. Bills arriving all at once. Bank managers getting uneasy.'

Jenni could honestly say she had never experienced any of those difficulties, but it hardly seemed tactful to say so. She had found that most men didn't like a woman to be more successful.

'What made an attractive girl like you go in for the business?' Clay Cunningham asked. There was nothing smarmy about the compliment and he seemed genuinely interested.

'I suppose you could say it was in my blood.' Jenni couldn't remember a time when she hadn't been interested in old things. Even as a child she had been fascinated by her grandparents' shop, asking nothing better in holiday time than to be allowed to help there, even in the most menial capacity. She had even spent part of her pocket money on the purchase of small antiques. The obsession had persisted into her teens and over the years she'd learned a great deal.

'Are your parents in antiques, then?'

'Heavens, no!' Jenni could laugh at the thought now, though once her parents' denigration of the trade had annoyed her. Then she sobered. 'They're both dead now. But in any case they weren't a bit interested. My father was a scientist. He got his degree at Oxford and met my mother there. She was a mathematician.'

Though Jenni would never have admitted it to anyone else, she had a shrewd suspicion that her mother—an arrant snob who had despised her in-laws for being 'in trade'—would never have married their son if he hadn't so obviously been 'going places'.

'So you'll have had a good education too.'

'Yes, I went up to Oxford.' Her parents had been adamant that Jenni, an intelligent child, should go to their old university. And Jenni, with unusual wisdom for her age, had held her peace. She had gone along with their ambitions for her while inwardly retaining her own, biding her time. But, unlike her parents, she was not of a scientific turn of mind. Instead she had opted for English and Fine Arts.

'So you have a degree? Aren't you rather highly qualified just to deal in other people's junk?'

'*I* don't think so,' Jenni retorted swiftly. 'Not if it's what I want to do.' It was her parents' old argument, which still had the power to rile her. 'No education is ever wasted. Why,' she challenged, 'are you an *uneducated* man, then?' She couldn't resist the thrust, even though she knew what the answer must be. Unless, which she doubted, he was self-taught, he had the accents, the social manners and the aplomb of a good education.

'*Touché!*' he said wryly. 'I gather it's a sore point.'

'Yes. I was always arguing about it with my parents. But my grandfather supported me.' Old enough when she came down from university to please herself, she had still been determined to work with her grandfather buying and selling the antiques she adored. She had been amazed when he did not immediately leap at the idea. 'But he said I should complete my education first by following a Works of Art course at Sothebys. By the time I finished that my parents had gone to America,' she told Clay, 'part of the brain drain. They were killed there in a plane crash.'

'Didn't you miss them when they emigrated?'

'Not very much,' she confessed. 'I was closer to my grandparents. My mother in particular disapproved of my spending so much time in the shop.'

'The shop?'

'My grandparents had a shop in Southport.'

'Had?'

'They're both dead too. They left the shop to me.' Jenni, as an only child, had inherited a sizable fortune from her parents and she had been amazed to find herself also the sole owner of the prosperous little shop and the flat above, together with her grandfather's considerable capital.

'So you're all alone in the world?'

'Except for my great-aunt and a cousin.'

'But if you're the owner of such an obviously prestigious business,' Clay said, 'why the market stall?'

Jenni wrinkled her nose consideringly.

'It's a good outlet for the less valuable items we acquire. When you go to auctions there's a lot of junk among the good pieces. And it pays its way among the less discerning customers. The stall is really Sonia's baby. I just go along occasionally, for a change of scenery.'

Jenni had only recently taken on Sonia—a distant and much younger cousin—as her assistant. Sonia, who didn't get on with her own parents, was happy to live in. And Phyllida Wallis, a schoolteacher who had taken early retirement, was glad to spend some of her free time in the shop.

'Sonia? That's the bubbly little blonde?'

'Yes.' Her cousin would be gratified, Jenni thought drily, to learn that Clay Cunningham *had* noticed her. 'And here she is now!'

'Whatever happened to the age of chivalry?' Sonia complained as she deposited a laden tray on the table. 'I had to literally fight my way to the bar.'

'I thought women believed in equal rights these days,' Clay Cunningham teased, and Sonia turned her attention to him.

'Well!' she exclaimed, and Jenni could have kicked her, '*you* didn't waste much time.' And, as Clay raised quizzical eyebrows, 'In getting to know Jenni.' Complacently, 'I said you wouldn't.'

'Sonia!' Jenni's cheeks were hot. 'Whatever will Mr Cunningham think?'

'It's all right, Jenni!' One of his large hands covered hers briefly, re-arousing those strange sensations. 'Your cousin is quite right. I *was* anxious to meet you.' His blue eyes, dark with sudden intensity devoured her face. 'Since that day at Ormskirk market I've found it quite impossible to get you out of my mind.' Somehow, a puzzled Jenni thought, he didn't sound as if that altogether pleased him.

His words had made her feel even more embarrassed, especially since Sonia was listening so avidly.

Clay Cunningham had finished his lunch by now, whereas the two girls had not even begun theirs. He glanced at his watch.

'Look, I have to go. I have to make an urgent phone call before the sale restarts. Can we meet again afterwards, Jenni—for a drink perhaps?'

Jenni hesitated.

'Go on, Jenni!' Sonia urged. 'Say yes, you know you want to.'

Clay was standing now, obviously anxious to be off. But his blue eyes were questioning her. Jenni told herself that it was only to shut Sonia up that she nodded an acceptance.

'I wish,' she told her cousin after Clay's tall figure had loped out of the pub, 'that you wouldn't put your oar in.'

'If I hadn't,' Sonia said with irritatingly undeniable truth, 'you might still have been dithering. You'll be thanking me later. All round, I reckon I've done everyone a favour.' A remark which Jenni was soon to doubt.

Back in the sale-room the number of buyers had lessened somewhat. The choicest items of furniture had gone just before lunch and only the smaller domestic punters were left to fight over the remains. Across the room Clay Cunningham exchanged smiles with the two girls. But, still surrounded by a little coterie of his own acquaintances, he made no move to join them.

It was nearing the end of the sale before the four oil paintings were put up. Since lunch Jenni's nervous tension had grown as one by one she ticked off the preceding items. And by the time the auctioneer was looking round for an opening bid her palms were damp with perspiration.

'Are those the ones?' Sonia asked in a penetrating stage whisper.

'Yes,' Jenni muttered *sotto voce*. 'But try not to look so keen, will you!'

The opening figure the auctioneer suggested was low, confirming Jenni's belief that he had no idea

what was coming under the hammer. She waited
until two or three bids had been made before she
joined in. The price rose slowly and one by one the
smaller punters dropped out until there were only
half a dozen contenders. These too narrowed down.

'Clay Cunningham's bidding against you,' Sonia
said in a tone of outraged disbelief, and Jenni darted a
glance in his direction. Sure enough she saw him
signal towards the rostrum.

'Damn!' she muttered.

'But I expect he'll drop out soon,' said Sonia.

But far from dropping out, Clay remained in the
bidding until only he and Jenni were left.

'If they go much higher it won't be worth my while
going on,' Jenni whispered to Sonia. 'There won't be
any profit margin. Oh damn, damn,' she said again.
'I *wanted* those paintings. And why did it have to be
*him*? It's going to ruin everything.'

It was obvious that Clay Cunningham did not
intend to pull out. It was equally obvious that he
knew against whom he was bidding. And finally,
when the auctioneer looked hopefully in Jenni's
direction, she shook her head. The final straw for her
was when Clay grinned knowingly in her direction
and lifted a hand in acknowledgement and victory.

'Now what?' Sonia asked.

Jenni had paid for her earlier purchases and was
making her way towards the rear of the sale-room.
She seemed to be in an unusual hurry.

'I'm getting out of here,' Jenni muttered. 'Come
on, before *he* notices we're leaving.'

'Aren't you going to wait for him? What about the
date he made with you?'

Jenni looked at her disbelievingly and made an
untranslatable sound.

'It's better I don't keep it.'

'What?'

'Oh, I know it's probably illogical of me,' she admitted. 'And if it had been anyone else who'd outbid me, I'd probably accept it with a good grace. But *him*! What sort of beginning would that be to a relationship? I don't think I could even bring myself to be civil to him right now.'

'You really think he's done you out of something good?' Sonia asked.

'Yes. The very fact that he was so determined to have those paintings confirms my suspicion that they were something out of the ordinary.'

'Then why didn't you go on bidding?'

'Because I couldn't be *absolutely* certain.' Despite her studies of the subject, Jenni knew she hadn't her grandfather's years of experience to back her hunches. 'I'd reached the limit I'd set myself.'

Jenni always made a pre-sale estimate of the ceiling prices she could afford. On auction day itself it was all too easy to get carried away and end up paying much more for an object than it was really worth.

As they left the building Jenni drew in a tiny breath of relief. But it was premature. Their departure had not gone unobserved.

'Jenni?'

She swung round to see Clay Cunningham striding after them.

'Hang on a minute, will you? I've just got to pay for the stuff I've bought, then I'll be with you.'

The utter gall of the man!

'Don't rush,' she told him coolly. 'I'm afraid I've just remembered a previous engagement.'

Her words stopped him in his tracks and for a moment he merely looked taken aback. Then his eyes narrowed and annoyance clouded his handsome features.

'Is that so?' he said with heavy irony. 'It's my guess you just thought that one up. You're piqued because I outbid you. That's it, isn't it? What did you expect me to do? Bow out gracefully because you're a woman and that would be the gentlemanly thing to do?' He laughed shortly. 'My dear girl, there's no room for sentiment in a business such as ours.'

Though at heart Jenni knew he was right, her disappointment was still too recent and besides, his sarcastic manner rankled. If he had said the same thing with even a hint of regret things might have been different.

'Exactly!' she said coldly. 'Which is why I'm breaking our date. Goodbye, Mr Cunningham.' She didn't wait for his reaction but turned on her heel. And Sonia, silent for once, followed in her wake.

# CHAPTER TWO

'WHAT a pity!' Phyllida Wallis mourned when Sonia—as always—regaled her with the day's events. 'But don't you think you were a bit hasty, Jenni dear?'

Secretly, Jenni was wondering the same thing. A few hours having elapsed since her defeat she was able to accept it with more equanimity. After all, why *should* Clay Cunningham have deferred to her in the matter of the paintings? He was quite right. Business was business. If she had had his number she might even have telephoned to apologise for behaviour that must have seemed very petty to him. She even went so far as to look through the local directories but not one of them included his name. Just as well, she comforted herself. Her approach might have been taken the wrong way. It might have looked as if she were chasing him. But she was still feeling regretful a week later.

As Jenni had told Sonia, she had decided it was time to go down to London again and spend a week there, rooting around the various street markets—Camden Passage, the Portobello Road, New Caledonian. And as she boarded the Liverpool to Euston train, she was aware of the usual frisson of excitement such a trip always brought. There was always that lovely feeling of anticipation that this time you might be lucky, that you might make the find to end all finds. And for the time being at least, this consideration pushed her regrets about Clay Cunningham into the background.

She might even take time out to do some clothes shopping, she mused as she settled into her seat in a non-smoking compartment. With her height it was often difficult to find anything she liked. So when in London, she generally made a visit to a shop which stocked everything for girls from five foot nine to six foot five.

With the slamming of doors, the train prepared to pull away from the platform. Jenni was glad her compartment was not too crowded. There were empty seats further along. No one occupied the seat next to her nor even that directly opposite, which meant she could stretch out her long legs and relax—even fall asleep if she felt like it. She had been up early to catch this train.

Knowing that the compartment would soon warm up, she shrugged off her thick winter coat, straightened her skirt and pulled down her emerald-green, polo-necked sweater. She favoured green a lot in her wardrobe, since someone had told her the colour was reflected in and enhanced her grey eyes. She pulled a glossy magazine out of the capacious overnight bag stuffed down behind her seat, and prepared to read for at least the first few miles.

At the last moment there was a mild commotion. Two late passengers had boarded the train with the consequent reopening and closing of doors. The first was a small, well-dressed woman who took a seat just in front of Jenni. Then long masculine legs strode past and a large male body subsided alongside the woman. He had his back to Jenni but she recognised him at once. What an unbelievable coincidence. Clay Cunningham, who had been monopolising her thoughts for these past few days.

Jenni felt an uncontrollable warmth invade and spread throughout the whole of her body. Would he notice her? Surely at some stage of the journey he must. And what would his reaction be if he did? Would he give her an opportunity for the apology she was ready to make, her admission that she had been in the wrong?

She tried to read her magazine. But though she stared at its glossy pages she wasn't taking in a single word. Every few minutes, irresistibly, her eyes were drawn to the collar of his heavy coat from which rose his nicely shaped neck and head. He was obviously travelling with the well-dressed woman and from time to time Jenni caught the occasional word of their conversation. It was easier to hear the woman's high-pitched voice than his low rumble.

'It's nice to have you back in England, Clay. Let's hope you don't have to go away again so soon.' Then a moment or two later, 'My goodness!' The woman's voice was decibels higher. 'You mean to say they could be Constables? Four of them? At a tin-pot provincial auction! But of course I suppose the local hick dealers wouldn't recognise quality when they saw it.' She laughed shrilly at her own witticism.

Jenni went first cold, then hot. Her fingers clenched on the magazine until her knuckles showed white. There was no doubt in her mind what they were talking about.

'Scarcely tin-pot, my dear Deborah,' she heard Clay Cunningham say. 'Southport has a very good reputation in the north-west for antiques. And most of the dealers know their stuff.'

Except Jenni Wallis, Jenni thought savagely.

'Even so . . .' The rest of the woman's words were

lost as the train rattled over some points. But Jenni had heard enough. He was sitting there, inches away from her, gloating over his success—a success that could have been hers. She could imagine, as clearly as if she could hear the words, his amusement as he related to his svelte companion how he had bested one of the hick dealers she had referred to, a girl whom only a few hours previously he had charmed into making a date. Fury replaced all other emotions. Thank heavens she hadn't been fool enough to keep that date. At least she had her pride intact.

They had been travelling for perhaps half an hour when an announcement was made that the buffet was now open for custom. Dry-mouthed with anger and shock, Jenni was longing for a cup of coffee, but there was no way she was going to pass Clay's seat. All desire to make her presence known to him had vanished. She would just have to wait for the trolley service.

Instead it was Clay who rose, bending to ask his companion for her order. Fascinated in spite of herself, Jenni watched his tall figure retreat in the direction of the buffet car. But then she took cover against his return behind her magazine.

It was impossible to escape detection entirely. As soon as the train pulled in at Euston she made for the nearest exit. But the slowly moving stream of passengers meant that by the time she gained the door Clay Cunningham was right behind her. She knew it was him without looking round. Her every nerve quivered with awareness of him. She had heard other women speak of the tangible aura that seemed to surround some men and knew vaguely what they meant. But she had never experienced it so vividly—until now. She jumped down on to the platform, stumbling slightly in her haste, and felt a strong hand at her elbow.

'Are you all right?' a familiar voice asked, then, 'Good lord! It's you! I'd no idea you were on this train—let alone in the same compartment. Where were you hiding yourself?'

Jenni's ankle was aching and so, unaccountably, was her heart. Though why that organ should trouble itself about this hateful man was more than she could understand.

'In the seat just behind you!' she snapped. 'Close enough to hear you bragging about the one you put over on me last week. I suppose you're off to Christies now to make a nice little profit!' She wrenched free of his supporting hand and hurried away along the platform, her progress frustratingly baulked by other city lemmings, still acutely conscious that he and his companion were not far behind. Despite the noise and bustle she felt almost certain she could hear his footsteps, long and measured. The back of her neck prickled self-consciously as she imagined him assessing her—unfavourably no doubt. Once through the barrier, she almost ran for the escalator down to the Underground and did not breathe easily until she looked around the crowded compartment and saw no sign of Clay Cunningham.

'And I hope I never have to see him again,' she muttered under her breath, annoyed at the tears that stung behind her eyelids, giving the lie to her words.

She had made a previous booking at the hotel near Russell Square which she always used when in London. And as it was the wrong time of day for the markets, she decided to deposit her luggage and cheer herself up by visiting a couple of her favourite places.

Every time she was in London, Liberty's drew her like a magnet. A series of labyrinthine Aladdin's Caves, its balconies were strewn with luxury, swathes of silk, rich patchwork quilts and Eastern rugs. Later, in Covent Garden, she wandered around looking at the stalls set out under the cast-iron and glass roof of the central market building and envied the stallholders their protection from the weather. It was a far cry from her exposed and draughty position near Ormskirk's clock tower. Also under cover—nearly an acre and a half of delicate Victorian glass roof—were arcades of small shops in elegant galleries, full of tempting wares. But somehow even her two favourite haunts could not charm her out of her mood of gloom. Chilled outwardly by the winter's day and inwardly by her disillusion with Clay Cunningham, she went in search of a hot drink and something to eat.

There was a basement restaurant she had patronised before, whose atmosphere of bare bricks and colourful posters advertising cultural events appealed to her. The lower floor was gained by means of a spiral black-painted iron staircase. Chairs of polished bentwood were arranged around circular wooden tables, set in intimate secluded corners.

Usually Jenni watched her diet. She didn't want her tall shapely body to run to fat in later years. But today she felt in need of comfort. The incident on the train had shaken her badly. She ordered a hot chocolate and fudge fingers. While she waited she looked around her at the mixed clientele coming and going via the spiral stairs. Businessmen in formal suits mingled with young men clad entirely in leather with spiky multi-coloured hair and . . .

Oh, no! It couldn't be. With all the places in the city to choose from it couldn't be Clay Cunningham descending the spiral staircase and looking round for a place to sit. A spasm akin to anguish ran through Jenni's entire body and momentarily she closed her eyes. When she opened them it was to find him standing over her.

'This seems to be the only empty seat in the place.' His voice was a deep, throaty purr from the cavern of his broad chest.

'Are you . . . are you following me?' she said faintly.

'No, as it happens. But our paths do seem fated to cross, don't they?' It was said with humour and yet Jenni sensed a certain wry displeasure. She stood up. But quick as a flash a large hand shot out and captured her wrist. 'Where are you going? You haven't been served yet.'

'I've changed my mind. I'm not hungry.' That was true enough—now. At the sight of him her appetite had vanished entirely. 'I'll wait till I get back to my hotel.' But if she had expected him to release her she was disappointed.

'Stay where you are and don't be ridiculous. We're going to thrash out this business of the auction once and for all.' He forced her back into her seat and just then the waitress came to take his order, blocking Jenni's escape still further.

While his attention was otherwise engaged, Jenni made a covert study of him, hungrily taking in details she hadn't noticed before—the square, determined-looking chin, the bold nose that widened and nearly, but not quite, turned up at the end. The waywardness of his fair hair. Liberally sprinkled with grey, it refused to lie sleekly on his well-shaped head.

How was it possible, she asked herself in vexation, still to be attracted to a man who made her so angry?

He caught her speculative gaze on him.

'What are you doing in Covent Garden?' he asked.

'It's one of my favourite places,' she said shortly.

'Mine too. Ever been to the Opera House?'

'No. I'm not keen on that kind of music.' She stirred restlessly. 'Look, Mr Cunningham, I'm not in the mood for small talk. I . . .'

'Nor am I. But I'm wondering just where to begin.' He leaned forward across the table, his manner earnest. 'I seem to have upset you pretty badly. Frankly, I'm surprised. With an intelligent face like yours I hadn't suspected you capable of pettiness. Surely you don't always win at auctions? So why the hostility where I'm concerned?' His blue eyes held hers steadily, demanding an equal honesty, and Jenni's opinion of him wavered once more.

'I *was* annoyed after the auction,' she admitted. 'But I'd got over that. As you said, I realise I can't possibly win every time. I was even prepared to apologise if we ever met again. But then I overheard your conversation on the train—about hick dealers. And don't tell me eavesdropping brings its own reward,' she said hastily, 'because I wasn't deliberately listening. Your *friend* has a very penetrating voice.'

'I see.' He continued to regard her with close attention and Jenni's cheeks began to colour under his intent gaze. Finally, 'I'm not going to apologise for outbidding you,' he said. 'That's just the luck of the draw. Nor am I going to apologise for the fact that I recognised the provenance of the paintings when you did not. What I *will* apologise for is any unfortunate remarks you might have overheard my companion make. I can assure you I don't share her sentiments. Nor,' he added with emphasis, 'have I at any time belittled *you*. Now whether you choose to believe me or not is up to you.'

Just then the waitress brought their orders, giving Jenni a chance to consider his words and formulate a reply.

'Well, Jenni?' he demanded. 'What's it to be? A continuation of hostilities or a truce?'

'A truce please,' she said a little shyly. 'I *do* believe you and I *am* sorry about the other day. The only excuse I can make for my bad behaviour is that I'd set my heart on those paintings and I was so confident of getting them.'

'A truce! Good!' A smile broke up his face into lines of wry charm, tugging at Jenni's susceptible heartstrings. 'I must tell you I would have been very disappointed in you if you'd chosen the alternative. Now, tell me, what are you doing in London? Business or pleasure?'

'A bit of both. But mostly business.'

'How long for?'

'A few days,' she told him. 'Long enough to visit most of the street markets.'

'Me too. Where are you putting up?'

She told him the name of her very exclusive hotel and saw his eyebrows rise. She waited for him to reciprocate and when he did she knew she had been right about his financial status. He wasn't very well off.

'So we could bump into each other again?' he suggested.

'Yes.'

It was impossible to tell from his tone of voice whether the prospect pleased him or not. But he went on, 'Then instead of leaving things to chance, why don't we arrange to spend some time together?' And, while Jenni's heart was still performing incredible gymnastics, 'What are you doing with the rest of your day? January sales?'

She shook her head. The sales, whatever time of year, had never been any temptation to her. She preferred to shop for clothes at exclusive boutiques as and when she wanted them, rather than buy for the sake of a doubtful bargain. When in London she liked to visit galleries and museums. When she wasn't poking around the markets with their ever-present promise of hidden treasure, the possibility of discovering some long-lost Rembrandt.

'So you'd like to be even richer than you obviously are?' he commented when she had told him some of this. Didn't he sound a little bitter, for a man who stood to make a small fortune out of those Constable paintings?

'It's not just the money,' she protested. 'I love the hunt and I love old things for themselves. I always have.'

Suddenly she realised that their conversation so far had been mostly about her concerns.

'You ask a lot of questions,' she told Clay. 'But you don't say much about yourself.'

He shrugged. 'Perhaps there isn't a lot to say. What do you want to know?'

'Well, for a start, are you a local man?'

'If by that you mean do I live in Southport, no I don't. But I *am* a Lancashire man.'

Jenni waited expectantly but nothing more seemed to be forthcoming. She had been brought up to believe it was ill-mannered to cross-question people about their private affairs. But she didn't believe she

had ever met anyone quite so reserved. Within
minutes of making your acquaintance, most people
were almost embarrassing in their personal
confidences.

'What part of Lancashire?'

'Preston.'

'Then what were you doing on the Liverpool to
Euston train?'

'Simple.' He was amused. 'From time to time I
have business in Liverpool and I quite often go on
from there to London. Do you know Preston at all?'
he asked.

'Fairly well. I've shopped there. We've had a stall
on the covered market once or twice. And Sonia and I
have done the rounds of most of the antique shops. I
don't know if I've visited yours or not.' Her grey eyes
invited him to elaborate.

'Very unlikely.' But, just as she thought this was to
be another dead end, he went on with deliberate
emphasis, 'I would definitely have remembered if
we'd met before.' And his brilliant blue eyes
subjected her already colouring face to an intent
appraisal. 'What is it about you?' he muttered almost
as if to himself. 'You're not exactly beautiful, yet . . .'

'Well, thank you!' she quipped, unsure whether
pique or amusement at his frankness were
uppermost.

'No,' he went on, quite unabashed, 'it's not beauty
in the accepted sense of the word. Taken feature by
feature . . .' and to her embarrassment he proceeded
to do just that '. . . you would be considered by some
to be plain. It's the combination of unusual features
with . . .'

'My goodness!' she exclaimed semi-humorously.
'You're making me feel like some kind of freak.'

'. . . of unusual features,' he went on as if she hadn't spoken, 'with that air you have of tranquillity, as if nothing or no one ever knocks you off your perch.' Little did he know, Jenni thought wryly, that *he* certainly had the power to disconcert her.

'You're an original, Jenni,' he decided. 'That's the only conclusion I can come to.'

As they continued with their meal, Jenni—half irritated, half amused—realised that, deliberately or not, he had directed the conversation away from himself once more.

Despite her protests, Clay insisted on paying both bills, with the air of one who would be deeply offended if she refused. If he wasn't too well off, she thought, he probably would have a touchy pride where financial matters were concerned.

'Well, OK,' she conceded, 'but you must let me pay another time.' Then, at the quizzical lift of his eyebrows, she felt the too-ready colour flare in her cheeks once more. It must have sounded as though she was reminding him of his suggestion that they meet by arrangement next time.

'You never did say what you were doing this afternoon,' he prompted her.

'I thought I'd visit the National Gallery. I usually try to go when I'm in town.' To her disappointment he didn't suggest accompanying her.

'And tomorrow?' he asked.

'New Caledonian Market.'

'OK. I have to meet Deborah—Deborah Clarke—this afternoon. You know? She was with me on the train.'

'Oh, I remember,' said Jenni drily.

'But I'll see you at the Caledonian tomorrow,' Clay suggested. 'All right by you?'

It was very all right by Jenni.

Jenni's study of the history of art had made her very knowledgeable, which added to the enjoyment she always derived from looking at paintings. But somehow that afternoon she found herself lacking in concentration. Continually, a man's face intruded on her thoughts, coming between her and the subject-matter. Clay's face. And she wondered with more than idle interest what his relationship was with Deborah Clarke.

It was bitterly cold next day, freezing and foggy, as she left her hotel in the grey half-light of a winter's morning, but Jenni, filled with nervous excitement at the thought of seeing Clay again, scarcely heeded the weather.

You had to be in Bermondsey early. Trading started at five-thirty and all the best bargains would have been snapped up by seven-thirty. Often a nice piece of silver bought in the pre-dawn gloom would be on sale again in the Portobello Road three hours later at three times the price.

Although Clay had stated confidently that he would see her in the market, Jenni wondered a little anxiously if they would manage to encounter each other in the crowd. It always amazed her to find so many people up and about so early. Officious market inspectors strode about, full of noisy self-importance. Traders with their tight-lipped henchmen, eyes skinned for pilferers, unloaded their battered old vans, disgorging heavy Victorian furniture and brassware. There were customers too, dim shadows moving about with torches, hunting for a bargain. Dealers like herself, drawn to London, the Mecca of the antiques world. Sightseers. And avid antique-hungry Americans betrayed by their loud accented voices.

'Jenni!'

She spun on her heel, heart thumping, unable to conceal the smile of pleasure at the sight of Clay's familiar figure.

'I'm surprised you found me,' she said a little breathlessly.

'No problem! You'll always stand out in a crowd, Jenni,' he told her and she was glad of the poor light which concealed her reddening cheeks. She wasn't used to men who paid her compliments at this time of the morning. Mostly they waited for a suitably romantic hour and setting.

He put a hand beneath her elbow, increasing her mood of soaring euphoria and together they made their way along the stalls shrouded by a mist of warm human breath, as would-be buyers peered at what was on offer and dealers haggled over the wares.

'What are you looking for?' Clay asked.

'I'm not sure.' But Jenni knew that out of all her favourite haunts, in this fast-moving street market she was more likely to make worth-while finds. Stallholders turned over such a huge volume of stock that even the most knowledgeable occasionally let a prize escape them. 'But I'll know when I find it.' She looked up at Clay, half teasing, half serious. 'And I hope we won't be in competition today.'

But his reply was completely serious, giving her a warm inner glow.

'So do I. I don't want to fall out with you again, Jenni.'

And indeed they managed to remain on amicable terms as they worked their way the length and breadth of the market, making small purchases here and there. Jenni drooled over jet, amber and coral jewellery, lovely old name brooches—'Bertha', 'Florrie', 'Mother', 'Ethel'—the names redolent of another generation.

Meanwhile, Clay, under the eagle eye of a Cockney dealer with the curls of an angel and the features of a prizefighter, examined silver teapots, carriage lamps and officers' dress swords.

'Are you done?' Clay asked at last.

Jenni nodded. She didn't want to spend all her money this morning in case she came across something else another day. It was full daylight now and time to think about breakfasting at one of the hot-dog stalls which also sold coffee or scalding tea in plastic cups.

But Clay had other ideas. He led the way to a small café in a street away from the hurly-burly of the market. He took Jenni's coat then shrugged off the heavy duffel he wore, which had made him seem bigger and more powerful-looking than ever.

'I'm going to have the full breakfast,' he decided, 'how about you?' And as Jenni nodded, 'That was expensive stuff you bought this morning. Obviously not for the market stall.'

'No. It's all for Serendipity. That's the name of the shop,' she explained.

'"The knack of stumbling upon interesting discoveries" as Horace Walpole had it,' Clay observed. And Jenni was aware of a small glow of pleasure at the literary allusion. She wasn't a snob, but she did like a man to be her intellectual equal, and so many good-looking men were spoiled when they opened their mouths.

He hadn't mentioned the previous afternoon.

'Did your meeting go all right yesterday?' Jenni asked him. She had been rehearsing the question, rewording it until it seemed to her that it expressed polite interest rather than the curiosity she really felt about his appointment.

'Very satisfactory, thank you,' was all he volunteered

at first. But then he relented and there was a twinkle in his blue eyes which told Jenni he wasn't deceived for a moment by her casual manner. 'Deborah isn't a girlfriend. She's my partner's wife. She's an interior designer. Nobby—her husband—and I are not just antique dealers as such. We get requests from people wanting to furnish rooms and kitchens with traditional antiques. So we handle the décor too. If necessary, the three of us will travel miles to find the right tiles and flooring.'

It was the first time Clay had really opened up. And even though it was about his work rather than about himself, Jenni listened intently as he described a staff of fitters and joiners, decorators and curtain-makers.

'But that sounds absolutely fabulous,' she enthused. 'I'd simply love to do something like that. I've decorated and furnished our own flat, of course. But to be given a free hand with really big projects!' Her expression became thoughtful. 'It's worth thinking about.'

Breakfast finished, Jenni fished her purse out of the side pocket of the holdall that contained her purchases. But as she started to open it a large square hand clamped down over hers.

'Put that away,' Clay ordered. 'This is my treat.'

'Oh, no!' she protested, 'I couldn't possibly let you. I owe you for yesterday.'

'You owe me nothing,' he insisted. 'The pleasure of your company is quite adequate repayment.' Blue eyes met grey in a long battle of wills. But then the contact deepened in intensity until Jenni became aware of an alteration in his stare and an unnatural quality in the silence. She realised too that his hand was still over hers and that its touch was causing her to experience the oddest sensations. With careful casualness, she withdrew her hand.

'Then I can only say thank you for my breakfast.'

'I hope it won't be the last we'll share,' Clay told her. His words, probably a polite platitude, instead of conjuring up a similarly prosaic occasion, made Jenni think of another situation under which a man and a woman might share the first meal of the day and she was glad of the need to dive beneath the table and put her purse away, thus enabling her to hide her sudden hectic colour.

As they made their way back to the Underground, she waited for him to arrange another rendezvous. Indeed, she had half hoped he might suggest they spent the rest of the day together.

'I suppose you'll be doing the Portobello Road tomorrow?' he said at last, on the juddering downward escalator.

'Yes, and Camden Passage the day after.' Then, too quickly she realised, 'Will you be going to either of those?'

'I'm not sure.' As the train rattled into the platform he raised his voice. 'If I get held up elsewhere I'll try and give you a ring tomorrow evening at your hotel.'

It was the rush hour and they were unable to get seats together on the train. At each station their compartment filled up still further until Jenni could not see Clay for the commuters standing between them. It was only because of his height that she saw his casual salute of farewell when he left the train. With a sudden feeling of panic, Jenni wondered whether he did mean to see her again. Or had he just been making a glib excuse? She knew so little about Clay Cunningham, whereas she had practically told him *her* life-history. *Would* he telephone her tomorrow evening?

# CHAPTER THREE

NEXT day, in the Portobello Road, distant glimpses of tall, broad-shouldered, fair-haired men had Jenni's heart lurching momentarily. But as the morning wore on it was obvious Clay wasn't going to appear. And her dissatisfaction was increased by her failure to find anything she either liked or could afford. It had been known for Old Masters to be picked up for a few shillings or for a Sheraton stool to change hands for a pound or two. But not today. At least not for Jenni. And the rest of the day felt similarly stale, flat and unprofitable, despite an afternoon spent in the Tate Gallery.

Sometimes, on her buying-trips to London, Jenni took in a show. But that evening, though she scolded herself for such ingenuous behaviour, she stayed in her hotel room, willing the telephone to ring. And when its shrill sound broke the silence she had to school herself not to snatch it up immediately.

'Hello?' she said breathlessly.

'Jenni? It's Clay. I'm glad I caught you. I thought you might have gone out. Had a good day?'

Normally she would have given an enthusiastic yes. Certainly there had been plenty to see. Colourful Victoriana, stalls of tangled bric-a-brac winking and glittering. And behind the stalls, dark little treasure-heaped shops spilling their debris on to the pavement.

'No! It was rotten, actually.' Then, 'I take it you *did*

get held up?'

She heard him chuckle.

'Is that why your day was rotten?' he teased. 'Because *I* wasn't there?' With uncanny perception he had hit on the truth. But Jenni's self-respect couldn't allow him to know that.

'I *was* going to say,' she told him repressively, 'that I didn't find a thing all morning.'

'Never mind. Better luck tomorrow, maybe.' Then, with a note of diffidence she had never heard in his voice before. 'We *are* meeting in Camden Passage tomorrow?'

Jenni thrilled to that word 'we'. But she deliberately kept her voice matter-of-fact as she agreed that *she* certainly would be going. And yes, she would see him there—if he made it this time.

'You're not offended with me, are you?' he asked. 'Because I didn't make it today?'

'Oh, no!' she said quickly. Too quickly, she realised, and was glad he couldn't see her colouring. 'I mean, it wasn't a definite arrangement. And . . . and just because our paths have crossed once or twice doesn't mean . . . I don't want you to feel you're obliged to . . .'

'But I *am* obliged,' he interrupted her slightly incoherent disclaimer. 'Very much obliged—to Fate for making our paths cross. Do you believe in Fate, Jenni? In Nemesis?'

She wished she could see his face. She wasn't sure if he meant it or if he was still teasing her.

'In Fate perhaps,' she said. Then, so that he wouldn't think she was taking him too seriously, 'But Nemesis? I'd rather not. Wasn't she rather an unpleasant female?'

'Mm. Daughter of the Night. Greek goddess of

retribution.'

'Well, in that case,' Jenni told him, 'I'll definitely opt for Fate. I don't think I've done anything to deserve the other lady's attention.' Then, half-seriously, 'Have you?'

'No.' But his voice was lower-key now, and Jenni wondered if she was just imagining the waves of depression that seemed to be transmitted along the telephone wires. 'But we don't always deserve our fate.' He was silent for a moment but when he spoke again she knew he had shaken off the moment of gloom. 'Anyway, I've given up trying to fight Fate. And at least she ordained *our* meeting.' Huskily, 'As I said, I'm very grateful to her for that.'

It was Jenni's turn to be silent. He had this uncanny power of rendering her completely tongue-tied. Again she wished she could see him, to gauge the sincerity of his words. Did he mean them? Or was he just shooting a line?

'Jenni? Are you still there?'

'Yes.'

'Are *you* glad we met? Don't be afraid of telling me the truth.' The bitter note was back. 'If you'd rather I cleared off, out of your life . . .?'

'Oh, no!' The exclamation with its overtone of horror was out before she could prevent it. 'No,' she said more calmly. 'I've enjoyed our meetings, our conversations.'

'Good!' It was just one word, but it was warmly said and this time there was no mistaking his sincerity. 'And I'll see you tomorrow. That's a definite arrangement this time!'

The moment she spotted him coming towards her, head and shoulders above the meandering throng,

Jenni's heart began to beat an irregular tattoo.
London, which yesterday had lost its charms for her,
today was imbued with all—and more—of its familiar
glamour. Despite her racing pulses she managed to
give Clay a composed 'good morning'. But she was a
little piqued when his greeting was similarly prosaic.

'Let's get started, shall we?' he suggested.

Camden Passage was closed to motor traffic,
preserved entirely for trade in antiques, crafts and
clothes. The tiny shops had an old-English country-
village look about them.

As Jenni had noticed before, Clay's methods
differed from hers. She liked to browse, examining
every corner of these veritable Aladdin's caves,
fearful of missing a bargain. But Clay seemed to
know by instinct whether a shop had anything to
offer him. Consequently their paths at times ran
parallel, then diverged only to merge again a shop or
two later.

It was on one of her solo forays that she made her
find. In a cardboard box which the shopkeeper had
obviously never bothered to unpack were some old
pieces of porcelain, their beauty and their identifying
marks obscured by grime. But Jenni had no doubts as
to what she held in her hand. Porcelain was rather a
speciality of hers. Adrenalin raced through her body.
Would the shopkeeper also recognise the value of the
pieces?

Over the years she had learned that there were not
many genuine experts about. How could there be, in
view of the thousands of antiques and collectables?
Few dealers, unless they specialised, were experts in
any one thing and not even the experts knew it all.

Ten minutes later, with the satisfied knowledge
that she had made a good bargain, she re-emerged

into Camden Passage.

'You look like the cat that got the cream,' Clay told her teasingly. But his gaze rested admiringly on her flushed cheeks and curving mouth.

'I feel that way!' Her grey eyes glowed warmly at him. But it was not just the thought of the treasures she clutched in her arms.

'I haven't done so badly myself,' he said. 'If you're finished, let's compare notes.'

She looked around at the jostling crowds.

'I don't want to unwrap these here. They're rather special and very fragile.'

'OK. Over lunch then? I know a nice little pub.'

'All right. But I'm paying for my own meal this time,' she told him firmly. And as he showed signs of arguing, 'I insist. Otherwise I won't join you. I don't want to be personal, Clay, but something you said gave me the impression that you don't find dealing in antiques quite as lucrative as I do.'

'Oh, there's money in antiques,' Clay said and there was that touch of bitterness in his voice that she had noticed once or twice before. 'But personal wealth depends on the kind of expenses one has.'

She waited for him to elaborate but he said nothing more. Instead he slipped a hand beneath her elbow and she was intensely aware of his touch as he steered her in the direction of the hostelry he had mentioned. It was a 'real English pub' and an antique buff's delight with its acid-etched mirror glass and crimson velvet button upholstery. Set out where the discerning could appreciate them as they ate were a host of Victorian relics. Warming-pans and carriage lamps rubbed elbows with carnival glass, while pairs of grotesque Nubian *torchères* stood side by side with wax-fruit compositions under sparkling glass domes.

'Fancy the shepherd's pie?' Clay asked as he seated Jenni in a secluded corner where she looked appreciatively around her.

While they waited for their food, Jenni unwrapped her finds. Clay's large hands were surprisingly deft and gentle as he examined the porcelain. With a spatulate fingertip he rubbed away some of the grime.

'Do you mind me asking how much you paid for this little lot?' he asked at last.

She told him, and as he rewrapped the items his mouth curled in the nearest she had seen him come to a smile.

'You're obviously a very shrewd young woman, Jenni Wallis. I congratulate you.'

'Thank you,' she said demurely.

'Do you have a customer for your porcelain?'

'No one in particular,' she admitted.

'I think I know someone who may be interested. Someone who'll be prepared to pay what it's worth. Give me a few days when we get back up north and I'll contact them and let you know.'

'Fair enough,' she agreed. 'And now, what about you?' His purchases didn't look very bulky.

'I've only bought one thing so far. But if I don't find anything else I'll be quite satisfied with this.' As he spoke, with delicate care, he removed layers and layers of tissue paper, exposing to her fascinated and slightly envious gaze a superb Japanese ivory okimono, an intricate carving of a half-peeled satsuma, incredibly realistic.

'Fascinating,' Jenni breathed. 'Beautiful!'

'Yes,' Clay agreed, but his keen, intelligent eyes were intent on her enraptured face rather than the treasure he held.

Jenni continued to stare at the okimono. Heaven only knew what he had paid for it but it wouldn't be peanuts. As she transferred her gaze from the object to Clay her thoughts were clearly revealed in her mobile expressive features.

'Yes, it *was* expensive. But it helps when you're using someone else's money,' he said drily. 'As you rightly surmised, I'm not a wealthy man.'

'What made you go in for antiques?' she asked impulsively.

He shrugged broad shoulders.

'You told me once that antiques were in your blood. It was rather the same for me. Except that it was my parents' means of livelihood. Only they didn't do so well at it as your grandparents obviously did. They managed to scrape just enough of a living to support themselves and their children. But there was nothing left over for luxuries.'

'And yet . . .' she felt her way delicately, 'you obviously had a decent education . . .'

'Only at a State school. I left when I was sixteen. We needed an extra source of income. My education as you call it was gained from private study, evening classes when I was older and could afford them.'

Looking at him as he was now, a self-made man, Jenni could only admire him still more.

'So if you needed another income you obviously didn't work in your parents' shop?'

'Only evenings and weekends. I got a job with one of my father's friends—a carpenter. I've always been good with my hands.'

Looking at them as he spread them out, for his own inspection rather than hers, Jenni felt a sensuous shudder run through her. Her grandfather had always said you could tell a lot about a man from his

hands. But whereas he had been referring to
character, her thoughts, irresistibly, turned to the
more intimate uses to which a man's hands might be
put. And she knew beyond doubt that her body
yearned for the touch of Clay's hands. But he was
still talking and she dragged her mind back from its
dangerous imaginings.

'My father was never very prosperous and
eventually he went into partnership with another
man—Nobby Clarke's father. And when my father
died I came in for his share of the business. And now
Nobby and I work together and as I told you, we've
progressed beyond mere antique dealing.'

'What now?' Clay asked as they left the pub.

'Back to my hotel to do my packing, I suppose.'
She waited for him to make some alternative
suggestion and when he didn't her spirits sank. The
end of her trip to London seemed to signify the end
of an episode that perhaps might not be repeated.

'Does that mean you're travelling back tonight?' he
asked.

'No. Tomorrow.' Then, after a slight hesitation,
'When do you plan to go back?'

'I haven't decided. I'm in no rush.' He said it
almost brusquely. 'It depends partly on Deborah.'
But then he went on, 'As it's your last night, will you
join me for dinner this evening? A farewell to
London, a celebration of our successful buying trip.'

Jenni looked at him searchingly. Was that all it
meant to him? She wished he would give some
indication of just how important her acceptance was
to him. She realised she had no idea if he wanted to
see her again once they were back in the north-west.

'Thank you,' she said slowly. 'I'd like that.' Then a

sudden thought struck her. 'But nowhere too smart, please.'

'I hope that's not a polite hint at my impoverished state.'

'Of course not!' Jenni was indignant. 'I just haven't brought the clothes for it. I always travel light on these trips, to leave room for the antiques. But since you mention it, I would feel happier if you'd let me pay my share. I . . .'

'No way!' he said emphatically. 'I may not be the world's wealthiest man but I can still afford to buy my dates a meal.'

His dates. Plural. Ridiculous to feel so depressed. Of course a man like this would know plenty of women eager for his company. Discerning women who put character before riches. And besides, Jenni was willing to bet that, with his sexual charisma, riches would still be a secondary consideration to most women.

She had spoken the truth when she'd said she'd brought no formal wear with her. And apart from jeans and warm jumpers for wandering around cold early-morning markets, she had only the skirt in which she had travelled. And somehow—despite her plea that they go somewhere inexpensive—a jumper and skirt didn't seem quite the thing for dining with a man like Clay. She could imagine how all female eyes would be on him and their scorn as they wondered what he saw in such an ill-dressed companion.

As she had the afternoon free, she decided to remedy the deficiency in her wardrobe and she walked the length of Oxford Street until she was almost hypnotised by its glitter of neon and glass façades. But it was in a side street that she finally found what she wanted. Something smart and feminine but not too formal.

The dress was a silky-look wrapover in a sumptuous shade of her favourite emerald green. Buying a dress, of course, necessitated the purchase of a pair of shoes and she was fortunate enough to find a pair in just the exact shade of green and with a medium heel which would not add too much to her height.

She returned to her hotel with just enough time to do her packing and shower before setting out again to meet Clay. It was ridiculous, she told herself, but suddenly she was as nervous as if she were a teenager and this her very first date.

'I thought you said you had nothing to wear.' They had arranged to meet in the foyer of the restaurant and Clay's eyebrows, a shade darker than his hair, quirked upwards in amused interrogation. 'That is a most becoming dress. You look very good in it.'

He didn't look so bad himself in a beige suit that set off his tanned skin, Jenni thought with that familiar lurch of her heart which the sight of him always induced.

'I decided to go shopping after all.'

'Hmm. But that dress wasn't bought in the sales,' Clay commented. His eyes narrowed as he subjected her to a further scrutiny, studying the cut and the material. 'You have very good taste. But expensive tastes, obviously.'

Jenni could have cursed herself for her lack of tact. But then, she told herself, cheap clothes never seemed to suit her. If they fitted in one place they looked dreadful somewhere else. She had always found them bad economy.

'Just part of the celebration,' she said. 'I decided to

treat myself for once.' She looked around the restaurant, hoping he would drop the subject. There was a small highly polished dance floor, she noticed with a sudden flutter of her stomach muscles. Would Clay ask her to dance? It wasn't that she was a poor dancer. For a tall, well-built girl she moved with poise and grace. It was the thought of being held in Clay Cunningham's arms. He was the most sexually attractive man she had ever met, and she was very much afraid he might sense her reactions to him—and she wasn't ready for him to do that. Not until she knew what his future plans were regarding their relationship.

'For once?' Clay had not been diverted. 'I've never seen you wear anything—not even on your market stall—that didn't look as if it had cost a pretty penny.' He certainly seemed to have a chip on his shoulder about money.

'Look!' Jenni leant across the table, her manner earnest. 'So I can afford to spend a bit on myself! That's just my good luck—an accident of this Fate you're so fond of talking about. But it's not appearances or money that are important when you come right down to it, but people. Would you like me any better,' she asked recklessly, 'if I were poor and shabby?'

'Jenni,' Clay's eyes seemed to caress her, 'you'd look like a princess in anything. But,' and now he was rueful rather than bitter, 'it would put you more in my league.'

Fortunately the waiter appeared then, with the menus, putting an end to the subject. And with their meal and a bottle of wine selected, Jenni sought for a non-controversial topic of conversation. What she wanted most was to talk about Clay himself. In some

ways he was very forthcoming, in others strangely
reserved. Why—a thrill of horror shot through
her—he might even be married. The thought hadn't
occurred to her before. And yet there was no way she
could bring herself to ask him a question like that. It
presumed too much on his intentions towards her.
She was startled out of these musings by Clay's
sudden question.

'How old are you, Jenni?' And as she looked at him
in surprise, 'Oh, I know it's considered impolite to
ask a lady her age. But you're young enough for it not
to matter. Twenty-two? Twenty-three?'

'I'm twenty-five, actually,' she admitted.

'You don't look it. And you're not married.' His
gaze flickered for a moment towards her left hand.
'And not engaged . . . or anything?'

Jenni shook her red head at him. It was incredible
how their thoughts so often seemed to run parallel.

'Not even "or anything",' she said with an impish
grin which, just for an instant, showed that oddly
engaging crooked tooth. But she blushed as he went
on,

'Are all the men in Southport blind?'

'I've just never met anyone I'd like to spend the
rest of my life with.' Until now, she added silently.
Then, mustering her courage—after all he had asked
first—'And since we're being so personal, are *you*
married . . . or anything?'

'No. I'm not married—or anything.' But whereas
Jenni had been able to answer him light-heartedly, he
spoke with that note of bitterness which seemed to
recur from time to time in his speech.

Perhaps he had had a blighted romance at some
time, Jenni thought. But at least, her heart sang, he
was free.

They chose a sweet course, followed by coffee, during which they covered more general topics, and gradually his dark mood seemed to pass. And then the moment she had half feared, half longed for was upon her.

'Would you care to dance?' Clay asked. 'All your movements are so graceful I would imagine you dance superbly.' He rose and held out his hand and Jenni quivered inwardly as she put her fingers into his.

In her time Jenni had danced with many men. With some it had been a more pleasant experience than with others. But never before had she experienced a reaction like the one she felt as she went nervously into Clay's arms. The moment he took her in his arms she was seized by wave after wave of inner tremors that she was afraid must be evident to Clay. He wasn't holding her particularly close to him, and yet the blood sang noisily in her ears as they moved slowly around the small floor space.

For a large man Clay moved astonishingly well. And they might have been dancing together all their lives, precision and timing coupled with effortless grace. The words 'made for each other' sang in Jenni's brain to the beat of the music and she moved in a state of silent, dreamy hypnosis.

'Don't you talk when you're dancing?' asked Clay after a while.

'Yes. Yes, of course,' she said a little breathlessly, 'if you want to.'

The slight agitation had not passed unnoticed.

'When did you last go dancing?' he asked.

'I can't remember. Why?'

'You seem a little out of condition,' he teased. 'And we're only waltzing.'

Jenni felt a wave of scarlet engulf her face and neck and she muttered something inaudible, lowering her head. But too late.

'Has anyone ever told you how delightfully you blush?'

'I don't find it delightful,' she sighed. 'It's a very embarrassing habit, one I should have grown out of years ago.'

'Don't ever grow out of it, Jenni,' he said softly, pulling her a little closer. 'Don't ever become so hardened by life that you can't blush.'

The increased proximity added to Jenni's agitation, and she wasn't sure whether she was sorry or relieved when the dance came to an end and they returned to their table.

'Another coffee?' asked Clay. 'Or a drink, perhaps,' as she shook her head. Then, 'Another dance?'

'No, thank you. I really ought to be going. I'm making an early start in the morning—the first train to Liverpool.'

'Well, in that case,' he gave in too gracefully for her liking, Jenni thought perversely, 'I'll see you back to your hotel.'

'There's no need,' she assured him. 'I came by myself.' But she would have been disappointed in him if he had accepted her assurance. He didn't.

'It's later now. The streets will be darker and emptier. I should feel happier in my own mind having seen you to your door.'

She wondered how literally he meant that and wondered if he would expect her to invite him into her room. She knew that if it was what he wanted she wouldn't refuse. Oh, only for a few moments, and all she would permit would be a few kisses. How she wanted Clay to kiss her, Jenni thought, and the pit of her stomach ached with the wanting.

But outside her hotel he bade the taxi driver wait while he walked her into the foyer.

'Goodnight, Jenni.' He was very formal.

'Thank you for a very pleasant evening,' she said gallantly as he seemed about to turn away and her hopes crumbled.

'The pleasure was mine,' he said gravely. Then, 'May I contact you when I get back? Ring you, or look you up?'

It was difficult to speak formally to disguise the joy that flooded her, and maybe her eyes at least betrayed her, for he smiled a little when she agreed.

'Anyone would think your trip hadn't been successful,' Sonia observed on Monday morning as they prepared to open up the shop. 'You're usually full of beans at the beginning of a week, raring to go. But today you look as though you'd lost a prime lot to Unscrupulous Ursula.'

Jenni had to laugh at her cousin's comment and in so doing shook off her silent introspective mood. Stupid to mope, when Clay had said he would be in touch.

'You approve of my finds, then?'

'Approve? You're the expert, kid. But I know what I like and this stuff's terrific.' But Sonia was not so easily diverted. 'So what is bugging you this morning, Jenni? Usually you're full of details of your trip, blow-by-blow accounts of how you knocked the vendors down to your price.'

'You know me too well,' Jenni grumbled. 'Well, I suppose I may as well tell you. Guess who was in London?'

Sonia's expressive little face ran the whole gamut of emotions from envy to incredulity as Jenni detailed the events of the past few days.

'So you made it up with him. I believe you really do fancy him, don't you?' said Sonia shrewdly when the account was finished. 'Seriously fancy him, I mean.'

Jenni nodded speechlessly.

'And has he fixed another meeting?'

'Well . . . not exactly. He said he'd look me up, or phone.'

'Do you know his phone number?'

'No,' Jenni admitted.

'Phew!' Sonia was derisive. 'You wouldn't catch *me* letting him get away without making some definite arrangement. I'd have had his address *and* telephone number.'

Yes, Jenni thought. Sonia, far less inhibited than herself, would have worked away with the unflagging persistence of a woodpecker until she had penetrated Clay's shell of reserve where his personal life was concerned. She, Jenni, couldn't be that pushy.

'Aren't you looking a bit fancy for market day?' Sonia asked Jenni one morning. Usually, in winter, all pretensions of smartness vanished in the overriding necessity to keep warm. 'Hoping Clay might turn up?'

Jenni flushed, aware of being caught out.

Two more market days had come and gone but though both girls were on the alert—Jenni covertly, Sonia more obviously—there had been no sign of Clay.

'Why don't we go over to Preston some time next week?' Sonia suggested at the end of the Saturday market as they packed their goods into the van. 'We haven't done the rounds over there for quite a while. And you did say he had a shop in Preston.'

Jenni knew her cousin was kindly motivated, but, 'No,' she said positively. 'I've never run after a man yet. If he wants to see me, he knows where I am.' Sadly, 'Perhaps he doesn't. Perhaps he was just being polite.'

With unusual tact for her, Sonia changed the subject.

'Are you going to that country-house auction over on the Wirral next week?' It was a weekly ritual to go through all the local papers, looking for announcements of auction sales, jumble sales and any other promising sources of stock. Sonia, with less knowledge and experience, did not often go to the auction sales.

'Wolverley Manor? Yes.' Jenni brightened a little.

Country auctions and house sales could be fun, even if they were full of pitfalls for the unwary. There was a lot of money in art and antiques. So it was very much a paying game to make copies of collectors' items. Furniture, of course, had always been copied. It was quite difficult to spot Victorian copies of seventeenth- or early eighteenth-century oak furniture, principally because the fakes themselves had now become antiques. All you could do if you got caught was to put the item in another sale and hope someone else was as green as you. But Jenni was not afraid to follow her instincts if she really liked a piece.

'I'll ask Auntie to come in for a couple of extra days next week,' she told Sonia. The viewing would take up one day, the actual sale the next.

'You'll stay away overnight, I suppose?'

'Might as well. It's less tiring than driving back and forth and it means I'm sure of being there for the early lot numbers.'

'I wonder if Ursula and her mates will be there.'

'Bound to be,' Jenni said. 'I've never known them miss a sale within a hundred-mile radius.'

'I wonder if Clay Cunningham will be there.'

Jenni was wondering that herself. But she wasn't left in doubt for long.

'There was someone asking for you today.' Phyllida Wallis was standing at the kitchen stove cooking their tea and she spoke over her shoulder.

'For me?' Sonia was always in demand.

'No, for Jenni.'

Jenni felt her legs begin to shake as her aunt turned around. There was a decided twinkle in Phyl's eyes and Jenni knew what was coming. Clay had been here and she had missed him. She had been in two minds whether to go to the market today. She didn't go every time. If only she had stayed in the shop!

# CHAPTER FOUR

'WHAT an incredibly handsome man Mr
Cunningham is,' Phyllida went on before Jenni could
ask any of the dozen questions that beset her. 'Really,
if I were twenty years younger I would have made a
dead set at him myself.'

'Phyl!' Sonia exclaimed as their aunt rattled on
further in this vein, and for once Jenni was thankful
for her cousin's impulsive nature. 'Stop teasing the
poor girl and put her out of her misery. Did he leave
any message for her?'

'Just that he was sorry he'd missed her.'

'Is that all?' Sonia squeaked, so ably expressing
Jenni's own frustration that it wasn't necessary for
her to speak. She didn't think she could speak
anyway. Disappointment was choking her. 'Didn't
he leave his phone number?'

'No. And before you blame me, I did ask. But he
quite obviously didn't want to tell me.' Phyllida
looked quizzically at Jenni. 'Are you sure he's being
absolutely straight with you? He's not a married
man, for instance?'

Jenni swallowed her chagrin and shook her head.

'No. I'm not a complete idiot. I made sure of that.'

'How do you know he's telling you the truth?'
Sonia demanded. 'A lot of men don't.'

'I don't know for certain, of course,' Jenni
admitted. 'But I believe him. There's something
about him—an air of integrity. I don't think he'd lie to

me.'

'Well, don't look so sad, love,' Phyllida comforted. 'If he's on the level and he's really interested he'll be in touch again.'

Clay telephoned that evening. It was late—almost midnight—and Jenni had given up hope.

'Clay!' It was impossible to keep the pleasure out of her voice. 'Phyl said you'd been in the shop. I'm sorry I missed you.'

He took her words and gave them a different meaning.

'*Have* you missed me, Jenni?' he asked.

'I . . .' she began and didn't know how to go on. Fortunately he didn't wait for an answer.

'I've missed *you*. I would have been in touch before, but a few problems cropped up.'

'Work?'

'No, not work.' And then, hastily, as if he feared she might question him further, 'Are you going to this big auction over in the Wirral?'

'Wolverley Manor? Yes.'

'Do you plan to stay away overnight?' And at her affirmative, 'Good. Shall I book us both in at the Horned Woman? It's very handy for the manor.'

'I . . . I could make my own reservation,' Jenni said. She wasn't sure what he had in mind and she didn't want any misunderstandings. But as always Clay was uncannily attuned to her thoughts.

'I was thinking of booking separate rooms you know, Jenni!'

'Well, naturally! I didn't think . . .'

'Oh, come off it, Jenni,' he teased. 'Tell the truth and shame the devil. The thought did cross your mind that I might be up to something.'

'A girl has to be careful these days,' she told him defensively. 'I . . .'

'Jenni,' his voice was amused, but throaty and tender too, 'nothing is going to happen between us that you don't agree to. Remember that. Now, shall I book those rooms?'

'Yes, please,' she said meekly. Her mind was in too much of a turmoil to protest further. He sounded as if he expected, hoped, that eventually something *would* happen between them.

'Do you have your own transport? I would have offered to pick you up, but it's not possible.'

She couldn't help wondering why. Aloud, she said, 'We have a van. I'll need that anyway if I buy anything.'

'Great!' He sounded relieved. 'I'll see you there.' There was a pause and she was expecting him to say goodnight and ring off. Then he said, 'You never answered my question. *Have* you missed me, Jenni?'

'Yes,' she admitted huskily. 'Very much.'

'Sonia! Sonia!'

'What on earth . . .! Where's the fire?' Jenni's cousin, jerked out of a deep sleep, was indignant. 'You larks have no consideration for nightingale people.'

'It's the van! It won't start. I shan't be able to get to the auction.' Jenni was up even earlier than usual, keen to get started on her trip.

'And, even worse, you won't be able to let Clay know you're not going, right?' Sonia hazarded, and Jenni nodded miserably. 'Well, don't panic,' Sonia went on practically, 'Let's think. Who else do we know who might be going? I know! How about Timothy? He owes me a favour.'

Sonia's boyfriend—one of the many—came up
trumps and a quarter of an hour later Jenni was on
her way.

She was always glad to be through the Mersey
Tunnel. The thought of being actually underneath
the river gave her a feeling akin to claustrophobia.
But from Seacombe it was an easy run down the
motorway to Ellesmere Port, where they struck off,
cross country, for Wolverley.

Jenni would have liked to spend the journey
dreaming of the next two days, savouring every
moment that brought her closer to Clay. But Timothy
Marriott was a talkative young man and his sole topic
of conversation was Sonia. He was obviously badly
smitten with Jenni's cousin. And since Tim was her
saviour it was only polite to listen to him and
sympathise with his desire to persuade Sonia to settle
down—with him, of course.

The ancient village of Wolverley and its manor lay
in open countryside beyond Burton. The village itself
was a delight to the eye with its pink and white
sandstone, thatched cottages, hundreds of years old.

'Drop me at the Horned Woman, please, Tim,'
Jenni requested. 'I'll drop my suitcase off and walk
up to the house.' She was hoping also that she might
meet Clay at the inn.

'Yes, there's a room booked in your name, Miss
Wallis,' the girl at the reception desk told her, 'but Mr
Cunningham hasn't checked in yet.'

It would be ironic, Jenni thought anxiously if, after
all, Clay was unable to make it.

Wolverley Manor lay in a quiet backwater, slightly
apart from the village. Jenni passed through the
wrought-iron entrance gates, supported by stone
pillars surmounted by the Wolverley Crest—three

wolves' heads above a crescent moon. The drive wound through green meadows grazed by cattle belonging to the estate farm.

It wasn't a very big building to warrant the title of 'manor', Jenni thought. It wasn't very much bigger than a large family home. In the thin winter sunlight it was a calm vision of honey-coloured stone with tall, multi-paned windows and slender gables. Massive oak entrance doors opened into a lofty oak-panelled hall.

Inside, high-ceilinged rooms fanned out from an oak staircase. Beyond this the whole place was a maze of passages with steps and short staircases in the most unlikely places. It was a feast of the unexpected, the arresting and the downright enviable. Jenni fell in love with it straight away.

How sad, she mused, as she always did on these occasions, when an old family line petered out and the estate, home and contents fell under the auctioneer's hammer. But such events of course were meat and drink to the dealers. And they had come from far and wide, she thought as she recognised many familiar faces.

She bought a catalogue and began a slow, methodical tour of the three rooms, making a mark against items she might decide to bid for. Sometimes Jenni deplored her statuesque height, wishing she could have been a pocket Venus like Sonia. But on occasions like this her build was a distinct advantage. You needed a bit of toughness and aggression to shove a way through the crowds—people searching for treasures and brown-overalled porters, marking their own lists as people placed reserved prices for next day.

'Got yer eye on that, 'ave you, love?'

Jenni looked up from her inspection of several lots of Imari-ware.

'Hello, Ursula.' Despite her distaste for the other woman and her methods, Jenni was always polite. 'I haven't made up my mind. I'm not convinced it's genuine. And if it is it'll probably fetch silly prices.'

But she knew Ursula wasn't deceived. This kind of remark was common exchange among dealers on viewing-day. It didn't do to show your hand too soon. Other comments might be 'nothing much here that's any good' or 'probably shan't come to the sale anyway'. These were things everyone said, without meaning a word of it. And she was glad when the woman wandered away. She didn't want other people to associate her with Ursula and her kind.

Jenni had brought sandwiches and around midday she ate them, then carried on with her inspection, checking furniture for woodworm, glass and china for chips and cracks. Sometimes of course a damaged item was still worth buying, provided the repair was not too costly.

'Jenni!'

She swung around on her heel. Incredibly he had come up behind her without her being aware of him.

'Hello, Clay.' She tried to affect a composure she didn't feel.

His eyes made a swift assessment of her and Jenni was acutely aware of her old jeans and sweater which she invariably wore for the dusty task of grubbing around salerooms.

He was casually dressed too. Old grey slacks and a navy blue shirt in light-weight wool. But it didn't matter what he wore. He would always look breathtakingly attractive.

'I was beginning to wonder if you couldn't make

it,' Jenni told him.

'I had to drop someone off for a hospital appointment in Liverpool. It took longer than I thought. Have you had lunch?' And as she nodded, 'I stopped for some on the way down.' He joined her on her perambulation of the room. 'Found anything interesting?'

'One or two pieces maybe.' Even with Clay Jenni couldn't shake off her habitual caution.

He chuckled.

'It's all right, my dear, I promise not to bid against you today.' My dear! It was only a small endearment, perhaps not even meant as such, but Jenni treasured it.

Clay was looking around him.

'I see the sharks are out in force.' He bent to murmur in her ear, his breath warm and intimate. 'Sometimes if I think they're getting things too cheaply I run the prices up a bit.'

'Isn't that a bit risky?' said Jenni. 'You might be left holding the baby.' And the unspoken words, 'and you couldn't afford to have that happen' hung between them.

'It's a knack,' he grinned. 'Stick by me tomorrow and watch.'

She fully intended to stick by him and, at the thought of being with him for two whole days, Jenni smiled. And when Jenni smiled it was an experience for the onlooker, the lips of her generously proportioned mouth parting to show her teeth, a lovely warmth illuminating her soft grey eyes.

Clay continued to look at her, and Jenni wished she could fathom the strange expression on his rugged features. He seemed to be standing peculiarly still. Then it was as if, with a strong effort of will, he pulled himself together. A muscle moved in his throat and he spoke in an oddly croaking voice.

'What did you think of the inn? Room OK?'

'Fine thanks.' She was glad of something prosaic to say. 'Have you stayed there before?'

'Yes, I know this area quite well. In fact, I've always thought I'd like to live in the Wirral.'

'Don't you like Preston?' She was surprised. Quite often men had a surprisingly sentimental attachment to their home backgrounds.

'I used to—as a child. We had a happy childhood. But my more recent adult memories aren't so good.'

'Well, this place is up for sale,' Jenni said jokingly, 'once the contents have been auctioned off.'

'More in your league than mine,' he said wryly.

'I expect it'll be demolished and the land used as a site for a new estate,' Jenni said sadly. 'Just imagine! Rows and rows of tacky little boxes replacing something like this.' She looked around her at the gracious proportions of the room in which they stood.

'You really care, don't you?' said Clay wonderingly.

'Yes. I can't help thinking of all the people, down the years, who've lived here—their sad ghosts.'

'You believe in such things?'

'Yes,' Jenni said slowly. 'I think I do. I feel that when a building has been loved—as I'm sure this must have been—that love must linger in some form or other, even if it only makes a house seem a happy one. And I feel this *was* a happy place.'

'I suppose, as you like old things, you'd be bound to like old places too,' Clay observed as they made their way through the diminishing crowd and out into the stableyard where the more mundane goods would be offered for sale. 'And I imagine you'd like to live here—or somewhere like it?'

'Oh, yes,' Jenni breathed. 'Just think what you could do with a place like this.'

'What would *you* do?' Clay indulged her flight of fancy.

'I'd have it decorated and furnished as it must have been in the old days, before the family fell on hard times. I'd have it so polished and gleaming that it would know it was loved again.'

'And what about the estate? And the outbuildings? Do I take it you'd want to go in for farming too?'

'Not on my own,' she admitted, her broad brow wrinkling. 'I suppose I'd need a partner who was interested in that kind of thing. I'd be more likely to make them into a centre for rural craftsmen, or a showplace to sell antiques.' Jenni's eyes were glowing at the thought. 'That would be ideal, don't you think?'

'Oh, yes,' he agreed. 'But the chances of my ever being able to do a thing like that are about the same as pigs learning to fly.'

There were several cars parked in the stableyard. Clay stopped beside a shabby old Bentley.

'Have you got your transport here?' he asked.

'No. Our van wouldn't start this morning. I had to beg a ride with one of Sonia's boyfriends.'

'Jump in!' He held open the passenger door. 'It's too early for dinner. Perhaps you'd like to take a look at the surrounding area. From the rear the manor has a splendid outlook.'

Once outside the estate, winding lanes took them out towards the estuary of the River Dee. At a quiet, isolated spot overlooking the marshes, Clay parked the Bentley. He shrugged on a heavy windproof

jacket and Jenni was glad of her own warm coat when
he suggested they get out and walk for a bit.

A strong, blustering breeze was blowing over the
marshland, and as they walked, heads down, into its
blast, Clay tucked a companionable hand through her
arm, steadying and guiding her. Its purpose might be
merely supportive, she wasn't sure, but at his touch
she felt the ignition of an inner flame that was rapidly
becoming familiar, associated only with him.

At last, both slightly breathless, they stopped to
look out over the marshes and to the Welsh hills
beyond.

'Give me the British Isles every time,' Clay said,
almost under his breath.

'Do you go abroad often?' Jenni asked,
remembering the conversation she had overheard on
the train.

His face seemed to close up.

'From time to time,' was all he volunteered.

From their elevated position, Jenni could see that
the saltings with their coarse, grey-green grass
stretched out into the estuary for at least a couple of
miles. And beyond the salt-marshes the yellow
sandbanks of the tidal stream gleamed golden in the
winter sunshine. Some were smoothly rounded,
others ribbed into fantastic shapes by the currents.

'We've chosen a good moment to see this,' Clay
told her. 'In a few hours it will all be covered by the
tide.'

'It's rather desolate-looking,' Jenni said.

'Don't you think desolate places are rather
romantic?' he asked. 'I have a fancy for them myself.
I like the Yorkshire moors with their overtones of
*Wuthering Heights*, and this estuary inspired Charles
Kingsley's poem ''The Sands of Dee'', about the

young woman drowned while bringing home the cattle. Do you know it?'

She nodded, revelling as she had before in his presence at the stimulus of an educated companion.

'It's a treacherous place all right,' Clay went on. He pointed to the wide creeks and gutters winding through the marsh. In their muddy depths the sky was reflected—a strange, steely blue. 'The tide fills these gullies long before the marsh itself is covered. Deathtraps for unwary strangers. Or for straying sheep.'

'How far up does the water come?' Jenni asked.

'Not as far as where we're standing, unless there's an exceptionally high tide. But once upon a time Chester, Shotwick and Burton were ports.' He turned her round, his hands on her shoulders, to look back inland. 'There's the rear of Wolverley Manor. So you can see this is the outlook the owner of the manor house has all year round. I could live with this view.' He pulled her back against his chest and looked down into her face made rosy by the cold winter wind, and something more. 'Ready to turn back?'

She wasn't. Despite the cold weather, she felt she could have gone on walking with him like this for miles, in this easy intimacy of mind. But she nodded agreement.

Jenni was glad as she showered before dinner that she had packed the emerald-green dress she had bought in London. She was aware that it suited her colouring and emphasised the generous shapeliness of her tall body. And Clay's gaze only confirmed what she already knew. His blue eyes were blatantly admiring.

'It's very imaginative catering for a small country hotel.' To hide her confusion, she had pretended an intense interest in the menu which swiftly became real.

'Gloria and Bill Hughes used to work up at the big house in its palmier days,' Clay explained. 'She was the housekeeper and he was the chef. They didn't want to leave the area, so when this place came up for sale they decided to buy it. Surprisingly, their prices aren't exorbitant and . . .' he nodded towards the other diners, 'people come from miles around to eat here. Unless you're a resident, you have to book weeks in advance.'

'I wonder why the "Horned Woman"?' Jenni mused. 'There's a lot of repetition up and down the country in pub signs, but I don't think I've ever come across that one before.'

'It's a local legend. Mary Davies of Shotwick, not far from here, was the Horned Woman of Cheshire. She was said to have been born with strange excrescences on her head which grew into ram's horns, which she shed and regrew at intervals. Like everywhere else in England, Cheshire and the Wirral have their own fascinating legends.'

Following Clay's suggestions, Jenni tried Bill Hughes' speciality, spinach mousse with mustard hollandaise, followed by chicken breast 'Gloria' with dried apricots, smoked ham and rosemary.'

'That was a feast fit for a king,' she said as they lingered over their coffee. 'But very filling. I don't usually eat that much at night.'

'It won't do you any harm. You're a big girl,' he teased. And then, hastily, with an anxious glance at her, 'I don't mean that in any derogatory sense. As far as you're concerned, big is beautiful.' Soberly, so that she had no doubt of his sincerity, 'You really are a most attractive woman, Jenni Wallis.'

It wasn't the first compliment he had paid her, but Jenni felt herself blushing as usual.

'Thank you,' she said a little awkwardly. Usually she found it possible to accept compliments with grace. But Clay's obvious sincerity made her feel both uncomfortable and inordinately gratified at the same time. In a purely nervous reflex action she looked at her watch and noted that it was still too early to go to bed.

'Now,' Clay said humorously, 'you're not planning to run out on me, just because I believe in saying what I think?'

'It wasn't that,' she denied untruthfully. 'I was just thinking about tomorrow. I'm really looking forward to the auction. But it's hours away yet.'

'Hours that will pass more quickly in congenial company. The only problem with staying in the countryside is that there's little or no evening entertainment. I just have to make a phone call, then I'll get you a drink and we'll take them into the residents' lounge.'

Clay seemed always to have to make urgent telephone calls while he was away. If he hadn't reassured her that he was single, Jenni reflected, she would have suspected a demanding wife in the background.

The small room, attractively furnished with old but comfortable-looking chairs and sofas and a large, clumsy sideboard, was empty except for themselves.

'It doesn't look as if there's anyone else staying here,' Clay observed as he switched on the television, the room's only concession to modernity. 'It's the wrong time of year for holidaymakers, of course . . .

fortunately for us.' With a luxurious grunt of pleasure, he lowered his long body on to a chintz-upholstered sofa which commanded the best view of the screen. 'Don't sit right over there,' he adjured, as Jenni made for a matching armchair in the corner. 'You won't be able to see a thing. Sit here.' He patted the space beside him. 'There's plenty of room for both of us.'

With a churning sensation in her stomach, Jenni obeyed. It was a gambit with which she was familiar. It was one many men employed. The next move was an arm draped casually across the back of the sofa which would eventually find its way around the woman's shoulder. And then . . . she swallowed nervously as her imagination took her through the sequence of events to the moment when he would inevitably kiss her.

But she might have known that Clay Cunningham would be different from other men. He made no such moves. Though she was sharply conscious of his masculinity only inches away from her, he made no attempt to close that gap. Instead his attention appeared to be fully concentrated on the documentary programme. Perhaps this tension that seemed to quiver between them was all in her own mind, she thought wistfully.

The programme ended, gave way to a news broadcast. Jenni was only half listening. She had seen most of the news items once already today and as always it had been a catalogue of disasters. She picked up a glossy magazine from a nearby table and began to flick idly through its pages. But her mind was not on what she read. She was alone with Clay. All the circumstances seemed to be in favour of a deepening of their relationship and all he could do was watch television. She wondered he couldn't feel the impatience that rode her, stirring strange, unfamiliar sensations in her loins.

'Look at that!' Clay's hand grasped her arm and Jenni started, her heart racing. His touch, desired yet unexpected, had shaken her badly. But he seemed unaware of her nervous reaction. 'Isn't that really something?' he demanded.

Jenni fought to control her quivering nerves and looked at the television screen which was showing an auction room—Sothebys. The newscaster was reeling off facts and figures about a painting which had just brought a record price, but for the moment she was totally incapable of assimilating the details. What kind of state would she have been in if he had attempted to kiss her, when just this slightest contact with him had totally unnerved her? She tried to concentrate on what the newscaster was saying.

'The owner found the picture in the attic when he was clearing a house after a bereavement. A friend persuaded him to take it to an Antiques Roadshow and the expert there advised him to take it to Sothebys.'

'It's everyone's dream to make a find like that!' Clay exclaimed.

'I thought I had, remember?' Jenni couldn't resist saying. 'What *did* happen to those paintings?'

'I took them down to London, for an expert opinion. I haven't heard anything yet.' His grip tightened and Jenni moved restlessly. Only then did Clay seem to realise he was still grasping her arm.

'Sorry! Did I hurt you, grabbing you like that? You were reading and I didn't want you to miss it. I hope I haven't bruised your arm.'

'It's all right,' she assured him hastily, as he

seemed to be on the point of rolling up the sleeve of her dress to investigate. He might not have bruised her, but he had left an indelible impression upon her soft flesh, one which would take a long time to erase. She could still feel the tingling warmth of his hand.

'Are you sure?' There was still concern in his deep voice and in his bright blue eyes, and as had happened before Jenni found herself quite unable to look away from their brilliance. He went on ruefully, 'I'm told I don't know my own strength.'

'I'm . . .' she had to stop, clear her throat and start again, 'I'm sure.'

'Then what's troubling you? You look . . . oh, I don't know. But something's wrong.'

'No, nothing's wrong. Why should it be?' She stood up. 'I expect I just look tired,' she improvised. 'And as it's going to be another long day tomorrow, I'd better . . .'

'I know what it is!' Clay interrupted. 'It's those damned paintings, isn't it? Curse it! Why did I have to watch that news broadcast,' he demanded glumly, 'and remind you that you had a grudge against me?'

'But I don't,' she assured him hastily. 'You know I don't. We cleared that up days ago.'

'Then . . .? Ah! I see.' There was amusement in Clay's voice now. 'I knew I'd seen that look on your face before. Of course I have. You're running away from me, aren't you? You thought I was about to make a pass at you.'

'No,' she said again. 'Of course not. I know you wouldn't . . .' She stopped. He thought she would have objected, whereas on the contrary . . .

'You know nothing of the kind.' There was a kind of muted anger in his tone as he too rose from the sofa. 'You know nothing about me.' He was only a foot away and an incautious, purely reflex move on her part had brought her up against the vast sideboard. 'What would you do, Jenni, I wonder, if I *did* kiss you?' His eyes were on her quivering mouth as he leaned nearer.

Now that it seemed likely to happen she was afraid, filled with apprehension. She had a feeling that, once she'd been kissed by Clay, there would be no going back. She would know for certain just how she felt about him and any remaining peace of mind would be destroyed. She wasn't sure after all that she was ready to know the truth.

'I . . . I have to know someone very well, be sure that I like them a lot, before I enjoy being kissed.'

'You always do it that way around?' She stared at him uncomprehendingly. 'Why not try living dangerously for once?' he suggested with a decided twinkle in his eyes. 'Why not try kissing a complete stranger? You might find it's just as much fun—more, perhaps.'

He wasn't a complete stranger and yet, in a moment of sudden panic, Jenni put out a defensive hand, a gesture intended to ward him off, but found it clasped in his.

'Clay, please,' she said faintly. 'I don't know . . . I . . .' Her voice faltered before the look in his eyes.

Then, suddenly, his expression changed, became remote.

'OK, Jenni,' he said. 'I was only pulling your leg.'

Somehow his words didn't convince her and, as she continued to look at him doubtfully, he seemed to realise he still held her hand. With a gesture of rejection he released her.

'Go to bed, Jenni,' he told her. There was a wealth of weariness in his tone and yet her intuition told her it did not come from physical fatigue. To her, the accents sounded more those of a man mentally and spiritually drained.

It was some time before Jenni fell asleep that night. The incident, brief though it had been, had left its mark. She was convinced that he would have kissed her if she had been more responsive instead of so ridiculously nervous.

Idiot, she told herself. Whoever would think you're a hard-headed businesswoman? Why couldn't you have acted with your usual maturity, instead of getting flustered like an inexperienced teenager? If you wanted him to kiss you, all you had to do was encourage him a little.

When she went down to breakfast next morning, Jenni was aware of a strained atmosphere between herself and Clay. Not realising they were together, the waitress had given them separate tables and Clay didn't suggest that she should join him. In fact, he barely looked up from his newspaper to mutter a greeting and went on reading as he ate.

Jenni felt sick with misery. Her breakfast was dust and ashes in her mouth. As soon as she decently could, she pushed her plate aside, drained her coffee-cup and left the room. Back in her room, she brushed her teeth, collected her handbag and set off on foot, much earlier than necessary, for Wolverley Manor. She didn't want Clay to think she automatically expected a lift.

Half-way up the winding driveway a car purred to a halt beside her. Clay opened the passenger door.

'Jenni!'

'No, thank you.' She anticipated his invitation. 'I'm almost there. I'm enjoying the walk.'

'Get in!' he said sharply. 'I have to talk to you.' She

was about to refuse once more when, his tone moderated to a peculiarly pleading note, he went on, '*Please*, Jenni!'

'Oh, all right,' she said albeit rather ungraciously and slid into the seat beside him. 'What do you want?' she demanded as the car moved on.

'To apologise, of course!' He sounded surprised that she should have to ask. 'About last night. I get moody occasionally. But I had no right to take it out on you.' The car slid to a halt in the stableyard and he turned to look at her. 'And these days I'm not at my best in the mornings either. Will you accept my apology, Jenni?'

It was not in her nature to bear grudges, and in a way it had been just as much her fault as his.

'Of course,' she said warmly. With a natural, impulsive gesture she extended her right hand, then found it and its partner enveloped in a strong warm clasp that sent a series of sensuous shivers through her. 'But . . . but what got into you last night?' she managed to ask.

His grasp on her hands tightened and his blue eyes were grave as they held hers in an unblinking stare.

'What got into me,' he said slowly, a husky edge to his voice, 'was that I *did* want to kiss you. But the idea didn't seem to appeal to you.'

'It wasn't that,' she assured him. Her pulses were leaping still and her lips felt dry. She passed her tongue swiftly over the lower one in an unconsciously provocative gesture.

'Then maybe I just misunderstood? Would you have let me kiss you?' Clay asked.

Jenni's eyelids fluttered but she managed to hold his gaze.

'Yes.' Then she waited breathlessly.

His face cleared and the tight lines of his mouth relaxed. He leaned forward slowly, oh, so slowly. Then, gently, feather-light, he brushed his lips against hers. It was the most fleeting of caresses but, every sense alert and quivering, Jenni craved more.

She relaxed against him and, had her hands been free, she might have plunged them into the thick thatch of his hair in an attempt to prolong the moment. But already Clay was holding her away from him.

'This isn't the time or the place to kiss you as I want to kiss you,' he murmured.

Jenni followed the sideways flicker of his eyes. Already the stableyard was filling up with dealers' cars and vans. In a few moments the sale would begin. Auctioneers liked punctuality. Gently she withdrew her hands.

'I see what you mean,' she said with a smile.

'But we'll find the place and the time, won't we, Jenni?' he asked in a low voice as they crossed the yard towards the auctioneer's rostrum, Clay's hand at her elbow steadying her across the cobbles. 'Won't we?' he pressed.

Her cheeks flushing, she looked up at him, grey eyes shy.

'I . . . I'd like that, Clay,' she admitted, and felt her cheeks turn from rosy pink to fiery red.

# CHAPTER FIVE

CLAY looked with interest at Jenni's glowing face.

'I could almost wish we hadn't a sale to attend,' he said softly.

There was a chill wintry wind blowing in off the river estuary, but it wasn't that which made Jenni give an involuntary shiver. At this moment she too wished they hadn't to spend these precious moments together at an auction.

But they had, and the auctioneer was just announcing the first lot number. They lingered a while to see how the bidding was going. There was nothing in the yard that interested either of them, just household dross and agricultural implements. But from these early items you could sometimes get an idea of how the day would go, the kind of money people were prepared to spend.

'Do you usually get to sales so early?' Clay asked.

Jenni nodded. She had learned from experience that choice, useful objects could often be snapped up cheaply both at the beginning and at the end of a sale. Most sales warmed up gradually and early arrivals who had surveyed the goods could usually make wise buys. Similarly, as the sale proceeded, many people left after buying what they went for and remaining merchandise often went for reasonable prices.

Clay urged her towards the house.

'The real opposition will be inside already, where

the quality stuff is. They'll have bagged the best places, so as to catch the auctioneer's eye. Besides I want to make sure all the items I've marked are still there.'

Jenni nodded understandingly. It wasn't unknown for an unscrupulous dealer to secrete a good item under a load of mixed tat and buy the lot for next to nothing.

At last the red-faced auctioneer mounted his somewhat precarious indoor rostrum and a new lot number was put up.

Clay, Jenni noticed, made his bids so unobtrusively that even she could not detect them, but the auctioneer never seemed to miss his signal and several lot numbers fell to him. After a while, Clay leaned towards her, speaking softly, his breath brushing her cheek, the masculine scent of him assailing her senses.

'I shan't get this next lot. I can't afford the prices it'll fetch. But you watch if you want to see a bit of fun. See that tall woman over there? The red-faced, choleric-looking one in the fur coat?' It was Ursula he meant. 'She'll be bidding for the ring today.'

At first the bidding proceeded calmly. More and more people dropped out as the large woman topped their bids. At last there were only two or three people left in the contest. But the price continued to rise steadily. And now the woman began to dart annoyed looks around the room, trying to see who was still outbidding her. Jenni held her breath as Ursula's colour deepened to puce and still the auctioneer was taking bids from Clay. But even to Jenni, close as she was, his signals were undetectable.

Just as Jenni was beginning to worry, Clay dropped out of the contest, his arm going around her shoulders in a triumphant little hug, and he murmured, 'That'll do for now I think.' He grinned. 'Better not give the old bat apoplexy.'

'Ursula deserves everything she gets,' Jenni said. 'But you had me worried for a while there. I thought you were going to get stuck with that furniture.'

'You obviously know her.'

'Yes. Sonia and I christened her "Unscrupulous Ursula". She goes to all the fairs. We often get the next stall and you should hear the yarns she spins people. Sonia says she could sell roast beef to a vegetarian.' Vehemently, she added, 'I hate to see ordinary innocent people being taken for a ride, thinking they're getting a bargain when they're not.'

'Is Ursula her real name?' Clay asked incredulously and Jenni chuckled.

'Yes. Rather inappropriate, isn't it? Ursula means "little bear". But with her build and that coat she looks more like a grizzly.' Then she sobered, 'And believe me, she can be just as dangerous as a grizzly. If she finds out you're the one who did her down . . .'

'I'm shaking in my shoes!' Clay said it so comically that Jenni, looking at him, laughed again, a full-throated laugh this time with the appealing little catch in it. But her smile faded slowly at the oddly arrested look on his face.

'What's wrong?'

'That laugh of yours,' he told her. 'It was the first thing that attracted me to you. It drew me like a magnet—that day at Ormskirk market—even before I set eyes on you. I've been waiting to hear you laugh like that again.'

Fortunately, for she was temporarily at a loss for words, the auctioneer called the next lot number, and as this item—a pair of Victorian oil-lamps—was one

Clay hoped to acquire for a client his attention was no longer on Jenni. But how strange, she mused, that they should both have felt that instantaneous attraction. She could only hope it augured well for the future.

Ursula and her associates also had their eyes on the oil-lamps, and for a while the bidding was fast and furious.

'Going, going, gone! Lot 150 to Mr Cunningham,' the auctioneer said in an aside to the furiously scribbling clerks, and Jenni witnessed a look of pure venom directed at Clay by the disappointed woman.

With a short break for lunch, the auction went on all day, the crowd visibly thinning until only the diehards were left.

'Have you done as well as you expected?' Clay asked Jenni as they left the sale-room, collecting a few more dark looks from Ursula as they did so.

'Not bad,' she shrugged. 'Predictably, I lost one or two pieces to the ring. But fortunately the kind of stuff I buy isn't of much interest to them. What really upset them was when you got the collection of pot lids.'

Clay looked at her quizzically.

'You sound as if that bothers you. They don't frighten you, do they?'

'Not exactly,' Jenni said. 'At least, not the men. But something about Ursula always makes me uneasy.'

'The female of the species being deadlier than the male?' Clay seemed amused.

'Yes. Fortunately I've never had occasion to cross her myself. And I hope I never shall.'

'Well, you needn't worry on my account,' Clay assured her. 'Though . . .' and his voice took on a familiar teasing note, 'I'm very flattered that you *are* concerned.' As they drove back to the inn, he asked, 'How do you plan to get your stuff home?'

'I'll have to come back for it. Sonia's supposed to be getting the van fixed while I'm away. What about you?'

'I'm having it delivered. If you give me a list of your lot numbers I'll have them put your stuff in with mine.'

'Thank you. That **would** save me a trip. But you must let me pay my share of the haulage.'

'I wish,' Clay said with a touch of irritation, 'you wouldn't keep rubbing it in that you're a rich, independent woman.'

'Not that rich,' she riposted. 'But independent, yes, and I insist!'

'And now for less mundane things,' Clay said as they drew up outside the Horned Woman. He turned in his seat to look at her, his blue eyes warmly caressing.

Immediately the previous evening's confrontation and their subsequent conversation that morning flashed through Jenni's mind. Her heart skipped a beat and she felt an insidious warmth invade the whole of her body. Once again her fast-moving imagination saw the whole scenario.

'L . . . less mundane things?' she queried.

'Such as what we're going to have for dinner tonight.' He said it without a flicker of expression, so that she felt she must have misunderstood the earlier insinuating tone of his voice.

As she showered and changed into the green dress once more, Jenni read herself a severe lecture. Stop jumping to conclusions, my girl, she told herself. Look where it got you last night. Nevertheless, it was on tremulous legs and with a beating, hopeful heart that she went downstairs to join Clay in the dining-room.

Over another mouth-watering meal they talked over the day's events and then moved on to other topics, as always finding many interests in common. They liked the same kind of books, the same style of painting, the same music, and in the pleasures of intellectual discussion she forgot to be nervous.

'Not that I get a lot of time these days for outside interests,' Jenni confessed. 'What with the shop, the market stall, fairs, auctions and house clearances, there's not much left over for leisure.'

'How about dates?' Clay asked.

'Occasionally,' she agreed. What she did not tell him was that since she had met him she had turned down every invitation. And when they took their coffee into the television lounge the conversation continued on this personal note.

'You asked me once if I was married,' Clay said as he settled himself beside her on the settee.

'And you said you weren't,' she reminded him, heart in mouth.

'I'm not.' His words came out clipped and jerky. 'But I was once. I'm divorced. Do you disapprove of divorce, Jenni?'

'Disapprove? No. Though I sometimes think it's made too easy for people. They don't seem to work at their marriages any more. Obviously in some cases there's a need for divorce. But it's rather sad, isn't it,' she looked at him earnestly, 'when people who must have once been in love—or thought they were—split up?'

'Sad? Yes, I suppose that's one way of looking at it. Though in some cases I imagine it's a blessed relief to all concerned.' He sounded so grim that Jenni looked at him curiously. It sounded as if his marriage had been one of the unhappier kind. 'To my way of thinking,' he went on, 'people should give a lot more thought to what they're doing before they rush into marriage. My parents would probably turn in their graves, but I think there's a lot to be said for an open relationship.'

'You mean . . . living together?'

'Yes. Or even a relationship where the separate parties keep their own establishments.'

'I see,' Jenni said thoughtfully. It was quite a common practice nowadays, she knew, but somehow she had never thought of it for herself, nor anticipated meeting a man who felt that way. She was aware once again of sadness.

'You're very quiet,' Clay said after a while. 'Have I shocked you?'

'No, but . . .'

'But you're disappointed in me, perhaps?' He reached for her chin and turned her face towards him. 'A little disapproving?'

'I . . . I have no right to be either disappointed or disapproving,' she said a little unsteadily. The slightest contact with this man seemed to unnerve her.

'But suppose I give you the right to pass judgement? Suppose I say I want us to get to know each other better? *Much* better,' he emphasised. 'Will what I've said put you off, turn you against me?'

Jenni swallowed. How ought she to handle this? Perhaps it would be common sense to avoid involvement with a man disenchanted with matrimony, who wanted no more ties, no more commitments. But, if she were honest with herself, weren't her emotions already involved? And if she

turned down his suggestion she might spend the rest
of her life regretting it.

A wry little smile twisted her lips. As most women
did, she suspected, she was already thinking it might
be possible to change him, and that one day he would
be so in love with her he would be ready to offer
marriage and all that it implied.

He must have read her thoughts, for when she
looked up to speak he forestalled her.

'I won't change my mind, Jenni,' he warned, 'so
don't think it. I don't plan to make the same mistake
twice. When I say no strings I mean just that. It's only
fair to let you know exactly how our relationship
would stand. And much as I'd like to know where *I*
stand, I'm not going to press you for an answer
tonight. Again, it's only fair that you should have
time to think about it.'

She studied him gravely, her grey eyes immense in
her troubled face. Never had she felt so pulled in two
directions. Her upbringing was all against anything,
to her, so unconventional. Perhaps she should say no
right away, that she intended to wait for a man
willing to give her his name. But could there ever be
another man for her like this one? She doubted it. For
she sensed that with Clay it would be possible to soar
to unimaginable heights of physical and emotional
satisfaction—if she were brave enough to take the
risk.

'Don't look at me like that,' he said suddenly, his
voice a rusty croak. 'Or at least say something. Tell
me what you're thinking.'

Being Jenni, she couldn't answer him any other
way than honestly.

'I'm wondering if I have the courage to do what
you ask. I hardly know you. We only met for the first

time—what was it—three weeks ago?'

'And yet,' Clay said softly, 'I feel as if I'd known you all my life.'

It was the same for her but she wasn't ready to admit it. She scarcely dared admit it to herself.

'Promise me you'll think about it,' he said.

'I'll think about it,' she told him. It was unlikely she would be able to think about anything else.

He moved so swiftly he took her by surprise, pulling her into his arms, one hand at the nape of her neck, so that even if she had wanted to she could not turn her head away.

But there was no need for restraint as the lines of her body softened to mould with his. And she shuddered with pleasure, desire flowing through her as at last his mouth covered hers.

He kissed her with an ardour that promised undreamed-of fulfilment, and within her every sense answered and surrendered to his demanding lips. Her skin prickled, her heart thudded a jungle rhythm and she found herself wanting him to do more than just kiss her. She wanted his warm hands on her body. She resented even the fabric of their clothes that kept them apart. All this she tried to convey by her response to his kiss. She was conscious of the tension in him, of the shudders that shook his strong body, his uneven breathing mingled with hers.

When he put her away from him, drawing himself away slowly as if he had to force himself to do it, she felt shattered, torn apart, her body trembling with unconcealed emotion.

'I said I wouldn't press you for an answer tonight, Jenni.' His voice was throaty, the words emerging as though with difficulty. 'But I didn't say I wouldn't try to influence your decision. No,' he held up one large hand as she parted her lips to speak, 'don't say anything now. Sleep on it. Tell me tomorrow.'

Sleep on it! That was a joke. Jenni had never found sleep so elusive. But just as she was, finally, on the edge of unconsciousness a knock on her door startled her into wakefulness once more.

When she stayed in hotel rooms Jenni always locked her door. Now she slid out of bed and pulled on her robe.

'Who's there?' she asked against the heavy oak panels. But her thudding heart didn't really need to hear the answer.

'Me! Clay!'

'What do you want?' But again it was a superfluous question. Jenni couldn't forget how aroused Clay had been and she guessed that his instincts had outweighed his promise to wait for her answer.

'Just something I forgot to say.' And her 'Won't it keep till morning?' brought an uncompromising, 'No.'

'Well, say it, then.'

'Do I have to bellow it through a three-foot thickness of door?' he complained plaintively.

Jenni chuckled, but she supposed it would be embarrassing for both of them if the Hugheses overheard what he had to say. With fingers that shook a little she turned the key.

Clay was clad only in a thigh-length towelling robe, and she stopped him on the threshold.

'Aren't you going to let me in, Jenni?'

'I . . . I think it would be better if you said what you have to say and then went,' she told him tremulously.

'OK.' He shrugged resignedly. 'It's just occurred to

me that I didn't point out the mutual benefits of the kind of relationship I proposed.' Then, as if he couldn't help himself he reached out and ran a finger along her jawline. 'What a determined chin,' he murmured. His hand continued its exploration down her neck, around her nape and into the mahogany red hair.

'What benefits?' Jenni asked huskily. His touch was making it very difficult to think coherently.

'That either—or both of us—would be free to end it at any time.'

'And that's supposed to be an added incentive?' she burst out incredulously. 'It sounds a very shaky foundation to me.'

'I was about to add,' he said with mock severity, 'that I doubt very much that *I* shall ever tire of *you*.' His voice dropped an octave, became excitingly intense and he pulled her closer. 'I've never met anyone who affects me quite as you do, Jenni.' He seemed to find it necessary to clear his throat. 'But you're a lot younger than me. I'm thirty-eight. The time might come when you would want to be free. You might meet someone nearer your own age. I want you to know, if that happened, I wouldn't hold you back. There'd be no scenes, no recriminations.'

If the positions were reversed, Jenni doubted that she could act with so much dignity.

'And you needn't fear that I would encroach on the independence you seem to value. There would be no questions, no interference with the way we spend our time when we're apart.'

'You . . . you mean you'd date other women?'

'No, I didn't mean that. I was referring to other areas of our lives we might wish to keep private.' And what exactly did that mean? Jenni pondered. 'I suppose you haven't come to any decision yet?' His hand had not ceased its subtle caressing all the time they spoke. He had moved closer, his body crowding hers and again she was aware of how little he wore. The pearly opalescence of her skin became flushed with pink.

'No,' she said tremulously, 'I haven't made up my mind.' Pleadingly, 'It isn't the kind of thing one can decide lightly.'

'Have you any idea,' Clay said, his voice low-pitched and throbbing, 'just how much willpower I'm having to exert not to take you in my arms and carry you back to bed? You're unique, Jenni. You have an elusive, disturbing charm. Do you know just how delectable you look in that nightgown, with that magnificent hair of yours streaming down your back? You should wear it loose more often.'

His words, his voice and the touch of his hand were undermining her willpower. Beneath her robe her breasts were palpitating with the unsteadiness of her breathing and his eyes were on that betraying rise and fall. She must send him away while she still had the strength to do so.

'Please go, Clay,' she begged. 'I really do need more time.' As she spoke she backed away and began to close the door. His foot prevented it from closing entirely.

'Just remember, Jenni Wallis,' he said, 'I want you, you dreamy-eyed witch. I believe we could be good together, and I think you believe that too.'

Then his foot withdrew. Jenni closed the door and leaned against it, much as she might have leaned on his strength. She was shaking from head to toe, caught up in the ravages of a fierce desire. Clay's visit had destroyed all further hopes of sleep that night.

Curled up in a chair, Jenni tried to put his proposal and her feelings into perspective.

At her age she was a free agent, not accountable to anyone else for her behaviour. There was no one to disapprove or to be hurt. If she decided to have an affair with Clay that was her own business. Once upon a time it would have been unthinkable but nowadays it happened all the time. Film stars, pop singers, television personalities. Many of them had 'lovers', or 'partners' as they were more euphemistically called, and most people seemed to find it an acceptable state of affairs.

She was pretty certain that if she turned down Clay's suggestion he would walk out of her life. And she knew from the intense value she attached to every second they were together that she wasn't prepared to lose him.

It was very difficult to decide something like this in a cold-blooded way. She could hardly sit and draw up a list of pro's and cons. All she knew was that she wanted to be with Clay for ever. That she couldn't visualise spending the rest of her life without him. She shivered suddenly, but not because the central heating had gone off long ago. With a weary sigh she crawled back into bed, no nearer to a decision. Fate had brought her and Clay together, or so he declared, she thought on a jaw-cracking yawn. Let Fate decide.

By now the management had realised that Jenni and Clay were together and the breakfast table had been set for two. Clay was already seated and he looked up as Jenni entered the room, his face lighting up at the sight of her. As she sat down, he leaned forward confidentially, taking one of her hands in his.

'I didn't sleep a wink last night,' he told her

throatily. 'I expect you can guess why.'

'I . . . I didn't sleep much either,' she confessed.

'I couldn't sleep because I wanted you, Jenni,' he murmured. 'Why couldn't *you* sleep?'

She felt the hot blood rush up under her skin. She could not be so frank in her admission.

'I . . . I did a lot of thinking. I . . .' But she was unable to go on. Another couple, arrived overnight, were at the next table and the waitress was hovering. Diplomatically, Clay changed the subject.

He had asked the previous day whether she would like a lift back to Southport and Jenni had jumped at the chance of spending a few more hours in his company.

'Are you in a hurry to get home?' he asked as they drove away from the inn.

'Not especially. I didn't give Sonia a definite time to expect me. Whatever's convenient to you. Do you have a call to make en route?'

'Not a business call, no. I just wondered, as you seem to share my tastes in so many ways, if you were interested in museums.'

'It rather depends on the museum.' Jenni's nose wrinkled attractively. 'I'm not very keen on Roman remains, and I don't approve of stuffed animals.'

'Ever been to the Lady Lever Gallery at Port Sunlight?'

'No, to my shame I haven't. Though I've always intended to go there some day. Strange, isn't it, how we go abroad and look around galleries and museums and neglect those on our own doorstep?'

'How would it be then if we take a look round, have lunch somewhere and I get you home for mid-afternoon?'

'If you're sure *you're* not anxious to get home.'

'Far from it,' he said with a bitterness that tore at her heart. How lonely his home-life must be. And yet he chose to keep it that way. Strange. But all she said was,

'Then I'd like to visit the museum very much.'

'Good.' For a moment his hand rested on her knee. 'I was rather afraid you might be annoyed with me about last night. You said you did a lot of thinking.'

'I think I ought to tell you,' Jenni said quickly, 'that I'm no nearer to making up my mind.'

'But the idea doesn't totally repel you?'

He risked a swift sideways glance, long enough to see the colour that stained her cheeks as she said in a low voice, 'No it doesn't repel me.'

Clay swore under his breath.

'There ought to be places on a motorway where a man can stop and kiss a woman. Remind me to make up for it later.' He chuckled. 'As if I'm likely to forget.'

Port Sunlight was a delightful model village built by a philanthropic industrialist to house his employees. Jenni exclaimed with delight over the dwellings built in the English half-timbered style. Arranged in threes or sevens, no two groups were alike. Each house had its own garden but in the American fashion there were neither railings nor gates. From the war memorial one looked down a wide avenue to the art gallery, a classical renaissance-style building.

'It was built by Lord Lever,' Clay explained, 'as a memorial to his wife.'

Inside the building Jenni moved in exclamatory rapture through a veritable treasure house of paintings, sculptures, tapestries, china and furniture, displayed in perfectly appointed settings.

'Lord Lever must have loved his wife very much to create something so lovely in her memory,' she said wistfully as at last they left the gallery and returned to the car.

'Yes,' Clay said, 'they were both very much in love. He wrote ''I always knew that, whatever might happen in the course of the day, the great event for her would be my homecoming in the evening.'''

'It must be wonderful to be loved like that,' Jenni sighed.

'Jenni!' Clay stopped in mid-stride, his hand on her arm, and she looked up at him, wondering at the intensity in the blue eyes. 'Jenni, love can be a strong emotion whatever the circumstances. What I'm trying to say in my rather clumsy way is that you don't have to be married to be deeply in love. Remember that. Believe it.'

Was he saying that he loved her? Jenni was thoughtful again as they walked on and she was less talkative over their pub lunch.

She had expected Clay to press her again today for her decision. And she wasn't sure whether she felt relief or chagrin when he said nothing as he dropped her off outside Serendipity and drove away with the most casual of salutes, without even fixing their next date.

'So Clay brought you back!' Sonia was rearranging the window display as Jenni walked into the shop. 'How was your trip? Tell me all.'

Not likely, Jenni thought wryly. Sonia, six years younger than her cousin, was a giddy chatterbox. She was the last person in whom Jenni could confide. Fortunately, Sonia didn't wait for an answer.

'How did you do at the sale?'

* * *

The pavements were thronged with umbrella-carrying shoppers in drab macs and squelching shoes. The buildings were grey against a weeping grey sky. The grey canvas tops of market stalls flapped with each gust of wet wind. Just by Jenni's stall water slopped and gurgled into the dark maw of a thirsty drain. The weather matched her mood. Three market days had come and gone and no word from Clay. Each new day that dawned, Jenni thought, 'Perhaps he'll phone today.' It wasn't good for her, this desperation for the sight and sound, the nearness of him. She was beginning to fear that he had thought better of his proposition or found someone more eager to accede to it. She was appalled by the intensity of the jealousy this idea provoked.

She moved to serve a hovering customer.

'Yes, I could knock a bit off the bookends, but not much. I have to make a bit on them.' She waited patiently while the customer dithered.

'Psst!' Sonia attracted her attention. 'Look over there!' She jerked her blonde head and, following the direction of her cousin's gaze, Jenni started violently so that one of the carved elephant bookends fell from a hand made suddenly nerveless. Fortunately it made a soft landing on a pile of paperbacks.

The tall, raincoated figure moved purposefully towards the stall and now the day was beautiful, the steady drizzle a thousand prisms of light. Without protest Jenni accepted the much lower figure her customer offered.

'Clay!' she mouthed his name weakly, soundlessly.

'Your aunt said I'd find you here.' Clay came round the side of the stall and ducked in under the canvas cover. 'It's good to see you,' he said warmly. 'I feel starved for the sight of you.' And his blue eyes were hungry as they subjected her to an intense scrutiny; Jenni wished she could have been looking more attractive. The old raincoat and woolly hat were not exactly becoming. But Clay seemed undeterred. He took her hands in his and began to chafe them briskly. 'Good heavens, girl, you're frozen,' he accused. 'You should wear gloves.'

Absurdly happy, Jenni glowed up at him. At that moment the weather and her cold hands were her last consideration.

'I've got some in my pocket,' she told him, 'but I can't handle the fragile things in gloves.'

'What you need is a warm drink. Can you slip away and have a coffee with me?'

'We have a flask,' Jenni said, 'and it wouldn't be fair to leave Sonia. She's just as cold as I am.'

But her cousin overheard this exchange.

'Go on, go and have a coffee with him.' And, embarrassingly audible, 'You know you're dying to.'

'Not a very good day for trading,' Clay observed as, his hand under Jenni's elbow, he steered her towards the nearest café.

'No, and those that the weather hasn't kept at home are only what we call "three 'p's",' Jenni said humorously. 'Pick it up, put it down and push off.'

A burst of amusement escaped Clay's strong throat and Jenni realised it was the first time she had ever heard him really laugh. A smile once or twice, yes, a chuckle even, but usually tinged with irony or cynicism.

'You do me good, Jenni,' he said as he seated her at an untenanted corner table in a window embrasure.

They were lucky to find seats, since the shoppers had been driven in off the streets by the inclement weather. It was lunchtime and the little café was crowded almost to capacity. The warm breath of the occupants mingled with the steam from urns and the cooking smells, steaming up the plate-glass windows, rendering the grey outside invisible, making their corner seat an intimate cocoon.

'What's it to be?' Clay asked.

'Hot chocolate, please. But we'll have to eat as well or they won't serve us at this time of day.'

Jenni watched him as he queued, feasting eyes which had been hungry for too long for a sight of him. She had almost forgotten just how physically arresting he was. He moved lightly, the way big men often did. Even his back view was attractive, the way his thick greying blond hair was cropped short, so that his head was covered with crisp springy waves. And Jenni recalled how its thickness had felt to her questing fingers.

'Slip your coat off,' Clay urged as he placed a steaming mug and a plate of cheese on toast in front of her. He moved round behind her and slid the garment from her shoulders. His hands lingered on her shoulders, deliberately, she was sure, and she couldn't restrain the small, sensuous shudder that ran through her.

'Goose walking over your grave?' he asked but his blue eyes were laughing at her. He knew very well the effect he had on her.

He removed his own raincoat. Beneath it he was wearing a brightly coloured sweater. She couldn't take her eyes off him. He had such an interesting, intelligent face. It was the face, she thought, of a man who had lived through good times and bad. For though there were lines of worry on his brow, there were laughter-lines around his eyes and mouth.

Clay was looking wryly at their lunch.

'Rather different from our last meal together. But then,' and his tone became serious, 'any meal with you would be a feast, Jenni.' He reached across the table and took one of her large but shapely hands in both of his. 'That's better. You're thawing out a bit. You know it isn't really necessary for you to expose yourself to the elements like that.'

'No, it isn't,' she murmured abstractedly. His fingers were caressing her palm in a most exciting fashion. 'But we rather enjoy it.'

'You'll get weatherbeaten and rheumaticky,' he told her. 'But enough of that. How have you been, Jenni? Have you missed me at all?'

She was beyond prevarication.

'Very much,' she said simply, her eyes limpidly honest.

'Good.' He was pleased. 'I'm sorry I haven't been in touch since the auction.' He frowned, and for a moment the worry lines predominated. 'One or two things cropped up. But we're together again now. That's all that matters.' He released her hand and allowed her to eat. 'You got your stuff from the auction all right?'

'Yes, thanks.' The van had delivered in the week following the Wolverley Manor sale, and the sight of her purchases had reminded Jenni with aching vividness of those two days in Clay's company.

'What have you been doing with yourself?'

'Not a lot apart from work,' Jenni told him.

'Still no other man in your life?' The question was asked casually enough but his eyes searched deeply and disturbingly, as though her answer was really important to him. And because Jenni disliked the dishonest way some girls deliberately aroused a man's jealousy, she answered frankly.

'I don't get much chance to meet any, except for other dealers. And they're usually twice my age—or quite unprepossessing.'

'But you don't find me unprepossessing, Jenni? Even though I am so much older?' His voice had taken on that throaty quality that always played havoc with her senses, and she knew that the delicate colour was staining her cheeks.

'You know I don't,' she said.

'We have to talk, Jenni,' he said with sudden urgency. 'Not here, like this. Somewhere we can be alone. I want to hold you in my arms. Are you free tonight?' And, with a consideration she loved, 'You won't be too tired after a day on your feet?'

Even if she were totally exhausted, Jenni thought, she wouldn't pass up a chance to be with Clay.

'No, I won't be tired. What did you have in mind?'

'A meal and a chat.' Then, meaningfully, 'We have a lot to discuss.'

# CHAPTER SIX

IT WAS still raining as they walked back to the stall.
The wind still held an icy chill. But for Jenni the sun
was shining, and the fact was not lost on her
observant cousin.

'Made another date, has he?'

'Tonight,' Jenni said with shining eyes.

'Well, thank goodness for that. Now perhaps you'll
stop looking like a wet week.' And then, with
unusual seriousness for Sonia, 'Jenni, don't get hurt,
will you? Oh I know I pull your leg rotten about Clay,
but I do want you to be happy. He seems very nice
but . . . well . . . he doesn't look very prosperous.
And he must have realised by now that you're quite
well off. You don't think he could be after your
money?'

'No, I don't!' Jenni said vehemently, but she
couldn't have explained why she was so sure.

The last couple of weeks had taught Jenni a lot about
herself and her feelings for Clay. She knew she
couldn't bear it if she never saw him again. And
when she had seen him today, towering head and
shoulders over the market-day shoppers, she had
known with a quiet certainty that it wasn't just a
physical attraction she felt. She was in love with Clay
Cunningham. Tonight he was going to ask her for her
decision and she knew she was ready to commit
herself.

Clay was calling for her at the flat over the shop. She was ready far too soon, a fact Sonia did not fail to remark upon.

'Let's have a look at you, to see if you'll do.' Sonia circled her cousin.

'Well?' Jenni laughed. But she knew she looked good. For the first time in her life she didn't have to deplore the fact that she was tall and strongly built. Physically, Clay was more than a match for her.

'That dress,' Sonia declared, 'is positively provocative. You'll need a judo black belt to keep him at bay. But perhaps you don't want to?' she teased.

The dress in question was a beautifully cut number in shimmering peacock blue—a change from her favourite green. But the colour did just as much for her, warming her grey eyes and complementing her vivid hair. The crossover V-neckline gave tantalising hints of the creamy swelling breasts and the deep secret valley between them.

'I'm dying to see his expression when he gets a look at you.'

So was Jenni. And then the doorbell sounded, making her start violently.

'I'll get it,' Sonia insisted. 'You stand there, over against the mantelpiece, so he can drink you in all in one go.'

It was Sonia's excited enthusiasm that was making her feel so jittery, Jenni tried to tell herself. But as Clay stepped into the room she knew she needed no such stimulus from anyone other than herself and her responses to him.

To Sonia's evident disappointment, he made no comment before her about Jenni's appearance. But there was no need. It was there in his eyes as he confronted her, and Jenni's eyelids fluttered down before the raw passion in his gaze.

'Have fun,' Sonia told them and then, predictably Sonia-ish, 'Don't do anything I wouldn't do.'

'How much scope does that leave us?' Clay enquired in low-voiced amusement as they went downstairs, his arm around Jenni's shoulders.

'Not a lot, I imagine,' she riposted, feeling light-headed with the joy of his presence, the intoxication of his proximity. 'Sonia's a lot more innocent than she likes to make out.'

'Has she got a boyfriend?'

'Several. She believes there's safety in numbers.'

'Is she going out tonight?'

'Yes. She goes out most nights. I don't know where she gets her energy. She's a real night owl.'

'Then we might have the place to ourselves when we get back?'

Jenni's stomach muscles contracted.

'Quite possibly,' she managed to say in what she hoped was a normal tone of voice.

Clay said nothing more, but his arm around her shoulders tightened.

'Where are we going?' Jenni asked as he ushered her into the Bentley.

'Liverpool. I know you're keen on Chinese food. And there's a splendid little restaurant I use quite often. A family concern. I think you'll like it.'

It was a quiet run from Southport, through Crosby and Bootle, then along the dock road into Liverpool. Giant cranes resting from the day's labours stood silent above berthed ships with exotic evocative names.

'I love the atmosphere of Liverpool,' Jenni told Clay. 'To me *this* is Liverpool. Not the shopping-centre or the touristy bits, but the docks, the Liver building, the feeling of history. I know the planners are only trying to improve the city, but I do hate to see some of the old streets being knocked down. I hate to see shells of houses with torn wallpaper flapping. I can't help thinking that it was once someone's home that they spent hours of effort decorating, that they lived there, loved there.'

'You're a real old-fashioned girl, aren't you, Jenni,' Clay said, 'in spite of your independent streak? You're the kind of girl my mother would have approved of. I hope,' significantly, 'you're not *too* old-fashioned.'

She knew what he referred to, but she wasn't ready to talk about that yet. Later tonight, perhaps, when the mood and the atmosphere were right.

'Is your mother still alive?' she said instead.

'No, nor my father, unfortunately.'

'Were you an only child?'

'No,' and as she was patently waiting, he added 'I have two sisters.'

'Older or younger than you?'

'One much younger.' The information came out in grudging short statements. 'The other the same age. We're twins.'

'Oh, what fun!' Jenni exclaimed.

'Is it?' It didn't sound as if he agreed, and without finesse, abruptly he changed the subject.

The restaurant in Liverpool's Chinatown was neither grand nor well-decorated. It was, as Clay had said, just a family affair where diners ate a beautifully cooked meal under the watchful gaze of the whole Chinese family: women, babies, old folk. In a room above the restaurant could be heard the clatter of the *mah jong* tables.

Jenni was glad she had eaten virtually nothing all

day when Clay ordered a veritable banquet. Starters
of *won tun*, sweet and sour soups, *dim sum* dipped
into chilli sauce. A second course followed, steamed
*sui mai* and succulent *har gow*, prawn and sesame-
seed toasts. After the main course, sweet and sour
king prawns served with fried rice, Jenni had to
refuse a sweet.

Over the meal, before the bland-faced waiter, they
had talked trivialities. Now Clay leaned forward.

'I have a proposition to put to you, Jenni.'

Now that the moment had come, panic assailed
her.

'I know,' she said in a voice that shook. 'But not
here, not now. Oh, Clay, couldn't we go on just a
little longer as we are?'

He reached out and caught the hands that were
fiddling restlessly with her napkin, folding and
refolding.

'Relax, Jenni. That's exactly what I have in mind,'
he told her, and perversely, disappointment flooded
her whole being. 'I realise I've been a little unfair.
But,' his eyes darkened smoulderingly, 'I want you
so much and it isn't easy to wait.' His grasp tightened
on her hands, but then he went on in a steadier tone.
'No, it's a totally different kind of proposition I want
to put before you.'

Jenni had never thought of herself as being
inconsistent. But now she had gained the reprieve
she had begged for she found she didn't want it.
Instead, she wanted Clay to sweep her off her feet,
carry her along on the wave of his passion, make her
irrevocably his.

'Are you listening, Jenni?' he demanded when she
had been silent for a long time. And then, as though
he caught something of her mood, 'We won't forget

about my other suggestion, Jenni. I haven't changed my mind. Far from it.' He continued to hold her hands as he talked and Jenni was more than happy to let him do so. 'I've told you Nobby, Deborah and I are in the consultancy business. Well, Nobby's getting near retirement age. He's a lot older than Deb. I've been talking to them about you and we wondered if you'd be interested in taking a share in our firm.'

'What exactly would that entail?'

'Visiting clients to ascertain their needs. Buying trips to supply those needs. The beauty of it is, you're spending their money, not your own. So within reason you're not hampered by financial considerations. You can bid against the Ursulas of this world. Some of our wealthier customers practically give us *carte blanche*.'

'But why me in particular?' Jenni asked. She couldn't help remembering Sonia's words, not that she gave any credence to them for a moment.

'Why do you think?' he said with a crooked grin. And then, more seriously, 'I need an associate I can trust as I would myself. And, Jenni,' he gazed deeply into her eyes, 'I'm prepared to trust you with everything I possess, my life, my happiness.'

Everything except his name. Jenni couldn't help the bitter reflection.

'I wouldn't want to give up Serendipity,' Jenni said worriedly. 'Apart from anything else, it's a family business. It means a lot to me.'

'No reason why you should. Part of my other proposition to you, if you remember, was that we should each retain our own establishment. But going into business with me could do your shop a lot of good. Our customers may want to buy items from your stock, and of course they'd pay the going rate. Well, what do you think?'

'In principle it sounds like a good idea.'

'But you'd like time to think it over?'

'Yes.' Half-apologetically, 'I suppose you think me a very indecisive person.'

'Not at all. I should think less of your business acumen if you didn't want time to consider. Consult your solicitor too, by all means. And now, shall we forget business and concentrate on enjoying ourselves? Coffee?'

There never seemed to be a lack of something to talk about with Clay. With other men Jenni had often found conversation drying up, becoming forced. She and Clay always moved naturally from subject to subject, finding few important differences of opinion. She was quite sorry when it was time to leave the little restaurant. But all the other customers had gone, and although the proprietor was waiting with patient inscrutability she felt sure he was anxious to clear away and close for the night.

'That was splendid,' she said as they drove home. 'But I've eaten far too much again. You're leading me into bad habits.' Then she went hot and cold at the thought that her remark might be misconstrued. It was.

'I hope so,' Clay said softly. 'But I hope you won't consider them all bad.' He leaned over and switched on the car's radio. BBC Radio Merseyside was playing a programme of classical music and the rest of the journey was made in a companionable, appreciative silence.

'Are you going to invite me in?' Clay asked as they drew up in the side street outside the shop.

'Yes.' She was glad he hadn't just taken it for

granted. 'But it's rather late and Sonia might be back,' she warned him.

But Sonia's bedroom door was still ajar, the bed empty. Jenni returned to the living-room. Now they were alone she was absurdly nervous. Clay was already seated on the large comfortable sofa, looking very much at home.

'Would you like any more coffee?' she asked.

He shook his head, his eyes subjecting her to an encompassing appraisal, deeply disturbing, strangely mesmeric and when he spoke his voice was deep and unsteady.

'All I want at the moment is for you to stop wandering around like a frightened kitten and come here to me.' He held out one large square hand and as though drawn by some magnetic force Jenni moved obediently towards him. He pulled her down beside him and put his arms around her so that her head rested against his chest. She could hear the steady pounding of his heart and wondered that it didn't skip erratically as her own was doing.

'Relax, Jenni,' he told her, and her name was a caress on his lips. 'You're too tense. I'm not so crass and insensitive as to leap on you straight away. I'm going to take my time teaching you to love me and we're going to enjoy every moment of it, both of us.' He put a finger under her chin and tilted it so that he could look into her face, into the grey eyes velvety with emotion. 'You're not afraid of me, are you, Jenni?'

'No.' All that frightened her was the strength and intensity of her own feelings. She loved him so much. In all her life she had never felt this way before, and she wasn't at all sure she could handle it.

'Then you won't take fright if I kiss you?'

Mutely she offered him her lips, her eyes closing as he lowered his head towards her. But he did not take her mouth straight away. Instead he moved his lips along the curve of her throat, down to the shadowy cleft between her breasts. Then, before she could protest at the intimacy, he had moved back once more to the line of her jaw.

His tongue stroked the outline of her lips which opened softly and sweetly below his, and with a little exclamation he began a fierce, passionate exploration of her mouth. Passion flared swiftly between them and they were both trembling long before his hands moved to cup the fullness of her breasts, his touch searingly warm through the thin material of her dress.

'Jenni, Jenni,' he whispered as her fingers tangled themselves in the thick vitality of his hair. He pulled her across his knees and she could feel his hard virile need of her.

Beneath his sweater he wore a thin shirt, and as its buttons yielded to her importuning she slid her hands inside, finding his chest muscular and sensuously hair-roughened to her touch. He was reclining the full length of the sofa now, her unresisting body pulled on top of him, strained against him for more intimate contact. His hands shaped her body with inherent mastery, following, learning every curve.

Sensuality, sharp and sweet, flooded her. She wanted him as much as she knew he wanted her. Oblivious of everything but this wild desire she shifted against him, shuddering as her body cried out for his possession.

'Oh, Clay!' In a rush of hungry passion she said his name desperately, wanting him to know her suffocating need of him. Tense with anticipation, she waited for him to coax her to total surrender. But he gave a sudden exclamation that was almost a groan. His hold slackened and he lifted her away from him, straightened her dishevelled dress and moved to the other end of the sofa.

'Clay?' This time she said his name on a questioning, disbelieving note. This sudden rejection was like a blow to the solar plexus. Her body, unfulfilled, still throbbed its demand.

'You obviously didn't hear what I heard.'

'No?' She had been oblivious of everything but his lovemaking.

'The sound of your front door closing. I believe your cousin is home.'

'She won't come in here,' Jenni whispered.

'Maybe not. But,' drily, 'the possibility that she might is very inhibiting.'

'We . . . we could go to my room,' Jenni said, amazed at herself. But he shook his head.

'No, when I take you, my Jenni, we are going to be very, very alone, for hour upon hour.' At his words and at the expression on his face her heart began to beat with a breathless urgency once more and she made a little move towards him but he was rising to his feet.

'So now I'm going to kiss you goodnight, my love. And then, much as I hate to do so, I'm going home.'

As he took her in his arms it was obvious that desire still rode him as much as it did her. For an instant he pressed her hard against his throbbing body and his deep intake of breath made her shudder as she felt the pulsating hardness of his masculinity.

'Until next time, Jenni,' he said. Then, with a hard swift kiss he was gone.

\* \* \*

Next time! But when was next time to be? Jenni brooded over her breakfast next morning. Clay's comings and goings seemed to have no regular pattern. He very rarely made pre-arrangements. And that's one of the things you'll have to put up with, my girl, she told herself grimly, if you agree to become his mistress. Mistresses have no rights. His mistress. She had never put it to herself in those terms before and it had an unappealing ring. But it was an old-fashioned word, she consoled herself. These days one said 'lover', a much nicer expression.

'Penny for your thoughts,' Sonia broke in on her musing. 'Though I expect I could guess them for free. Clay beat a swift retreat last night, didn't he? And there was me being all discreet and tactful. I suppose,' she went on, 'last night's events are on the secret list.'

'Not all of them.' Jenni smiled and gave her cousin a vivid description of the meal and the surroundings. 'And Clay's made me an interesting proposition. No!' she said hastily as Sonia's eyes became owlish circles, 'a business proposition.'

'How disappointing.'

Jenni repressed a rueful smile. If only Sonia knew! But it was as well she didn't. However Sonia's mock disappointment turned to doubt as Jenni gave her a resumé of Clay's suggestion.

'Are you quite sure he's not just after your money?'

'No,' Jenni admitted, 'but I'm reasonably sure. And you have to take some risks in this life. But I don't think this is a risk.'

'I don't suppose it'll involve me. It's you he's after.'

'You and Phyllida are part of Serendipity,' Jenni reassured her. 'What affects me affects you. And it's not as if Clay and I are talking about a merger. We'll still have separate establishments.' In more ways than one, she remembered wistfully. 'And even if we were merging I wouldn't discard you like an old glove. In fact, you'll probably have to take more responsibility for the shop if I'm going to be away a lot.'

'What about the market stall?'

'I don't know,' Jenni admitted. 'We might have to give that up.'

'Oh, surely not!' Sonia protested. If she were honest, she preferred the open-air trading. 'Couldn't we take on a part-timer to help Phyl here, so I could carry on with the stall?'

'Maybe. Let's wait and see. I haven't agreed to anything yet. And now we'd better decide what we're going to take with us to Gisburn on Saturday.'

With the growing popularity of antiques, it was quite possible to find an antiques fair or fleamarket going on somewhere in the county every weekend. But Jenni and Sonia restricted their attendance to one a month and at a different venue each time. The two girls always enjoyed a fair. Unlike Ormskirk market, all the other stallholders would be antique dealers. They bought from and sold to each other, and for the most part there was an easy camaraderie with much joking and bantering.

They left Southport very early on the Sunday morning. Apart from a milkman on his rounds and a dark-haired woman walking a lively golden labrador, the wet wintry streets were deserted.

'I know trippers and holidaymakers are our bread and butter,' Jenni said, 'but don't you love Lord Street when there's no one about? It feels as if it belongs just to us.'

'Is Clay going to be there today?' Sonia asked.

'I've no idea,' Jenni admitted. 'I told him we'd be there. But he rarely seems able to plan ahead.' She decided after all that it was time she prepared Sonia for what might be. 'But in any case we . . . we've agreed not to tie each other down, to remain free agents.'

Sonia shot her a suspicious glance.

'If that means what I think it means . . .?' And, as Jenni nodded a little sheepishly, 'Oh, Jen! And I always thought I'd be your bridesmaid some day. Don't you want to get married?'

'Of course I do!' Jenni said with sudden fierceness. 'But I'm going to settle for what I can get, Sonia. I have to.' She rather regretted her sudden impulse to confide in someone.

'Well,' Sonia said with equal ferocity, 'if he ever hurts you I shall have a few words to say to Mr Clay Cunningham.'

Once a coaching-stop where horses were changed and travellers took a mug of ale, the ancient market village of Gisburn lay between Clitheroe and Skipton. For a small place it had a large proportion of pubs and restaurants which attracted custom for bar meals and high teas, so the stallholders could expect a good attendance. There was an exchange of cheerful badinage and complaints about the weather as the dealers carted in their boxes of goods from vans and cars and set them out on the trestle tables.

The unpleasant Ursula was there with her partner, as small and weasel-faced as Ursula was large.

'Boyfriend not with you today?' Ursula asked Jenni in a venomous tone which showed she had not forgotten nor forgiven Clay's victory over her at the Wolverley Manor auction. 'He's riding for a fall, that one, and you can tell him that from me!'

The stall dressed to their satisfaction, the two girls ate a belated breakfast then took up their positions and waited for custom, which, initially, came in a mad rush, then petered out to a slow but steady trickle.

'Every time we do a fair I put on weight,' Sonia complained. 'There's nothing to do between customers but eat and drink.'

'You should take up a hobby,' Jenni retorted, looking up from the patchwork she kept for idle moments.

'Here's the genie of the lamp,' Sonia exclaimed, 'He seems to appear out of thin air.' And with heavy-handed tact she left the stall on the pretext of needing another cup of tea as Jenni smiled up at Clay, unable to hide the happiness she felt at seeing him.

He came round behind the stall and took the chair Sonia had vacated.

'Thought any more about my idea?'

'Which one?' Deliberately provocative, Jenni fluttered her eyelashes and it brought an appreciative smile to his face. Under cover of the stall he took her hand, caressing its palm, making her stomach muscles knot in ecstasy.

'Either. Both, preferably.'

'I'd like to collaborate with you,' she told him, serious now, even though his touch was working its usual havoc. 'But how do we go about it?'

'Well, first of all I suggest you meet Deborah and Nobby, and then come with me to see my current clients, have a look at the scheme I've drawn up for them. Once the décor is approved, my team of decorators can go into action.'

'But won't Deborah object? I thought she . . .?'

'You won't be treading on her toes. Our
part—yours and mine—will be to find the necessary
antiques.'

'OK. When do we start?'

'Have you got a free day this coming week?'

'I can arrange to have a day off, as long as it's not
market day.'

'Tuesday, then?'

When Sonia returned to the stall with her cup of tea
she was in a state of high indignation.

'Ursula's up to her old tricks,' she told them.
'There's a dear old lady desperate to sell some pieces
of china. She looks as if she hasn't two pennies to rub
together. She would be unlucky enough to pick on
Ursula.'

'I suppose the old bat is only offering peanuts as
usual?' Jenni said.

'Yes. I don't know much about china but even I can
see they're worth more than that. Oh!' She flopped
on to the chair Clay had politely vacated. 'I hate
Ursula. I'd like to see her taught a lesson.'

'How about you, Jenni?' Clay asked and as she
nodded vehement agreement, 'That's easily done.'
He raised his eyebrows at her. 'Care to join me in a
little bear-baiting?'

Sonia chortled at the play on words, but Jenni
looked dubious. She had an almost superstitious
dread of making an enemy of the fat woman.

'Go on!' Sonia urged.

Taking Jenni's hand in his, Clay strolled casually
towards the fat woman's position, a couple of stalls
away. The little old lady was listening with an air of
bewildered distress to Ursula's denigration of her
treasures.

'I'd be robbin' meself if I gave you any more for them old bits and pieces.'

'Excuse me,' Clay said politely, 'may I see?' Deftly he removed a jug and creamer from under Ursula's nose. He held the items upside down so that Jenni too could see the maker's mark and they exchanged speaking looks. Clay turned to the would-be vendor. 'Perhaps you'd consider selling these to me instead, madam,' he said courteously, 'since it seems they would be of more value to me than to this . . . lady.' The pause was infinitesimal but Ursula caught it, and her unhealthily chubby cheeks became streaked with angry blood as Clay named a sum three times as much as Ursula had offered, and the old lady stammered a grateful acceptance.

'I hate to part with them really,' she confessed. 'They belonged to my grandmother. But I've no one to leave them to and the money would be useful.'

Jenni was filled with admiration and her heart swelled with emotion at the gentle way Clay treated the old lady, insisting that she join them in a cup of tea while he inspected the rest of the items she wished to sell, and when the old lady left she looked much happier.

'I don't mind so much selling them to a real gentleman like you,' she told Clay.

'You paid her far more than they were worth,' Jenni accused him mildly as they made their way back to Sonia.

'I know,' he grinned. 'But I'll be able to sell them all right. Besides, she reminded me of my own grandmother.'

'I thought you once said there wasn't room for sentiment in this business,' she teased him.

Clay grimaced.

'True. But it was worth it just this once, to see the unscrupulous one's face.'

'Yes,' Jenni had to agree, 'but,' soberly, 'I'm afraid you've made an even worse enemy of her.'

On Tuesday the rain took a day off, the first for a long time. And it was an enjoyable drive north to Kirkby Lonsdale in the Lune valley.

As Clay had suggested, Jenni had gone with him first to see Deborah and Nobby Clarke. The business, she discovered, was run not from a shop but from their large comfortable home on the outskirts of Preston. Jenni had taken immediately to Nobby, a gentleman of the old-fashioned kind. She wasn't so sure about Deborah. But then, if she were honest, it could be that her view was still coloured by that overheard conversation on the train.

'Your firm's fame has spread a long way,' Jenni said when she learned of their destination.

'Nobby believes in advertising,' Clay said. 'In *Lancashire Life*, of course, and all the other county magazines.'

Jenni had been to Kirkby Lonsdale before and liked the ancient market town with its quaint irregular houses, the little passages and lanes with their odd turns and twists and picturesque corners. Clay's client and his wife lived in an old and grey stately home to the north of the town, on the west bank of the Lune.

Clay introduced Jenni as his prospective new partner and Jenni liked the Ramseys immediately. Unpretentious in spite of their obvious wealth, they were genuinely anxious to be advised on the best way to enhance their lovely home.

Following an earlier visit, Clay had prepared some

sketches and when these had been discussed and approved, the Ramseys insisted that Clay and Jenni stay for lunch. Mrs Ramsey collected papier mâché and after the meal she carried Jenni off to look at the assortment she had assembled over the years. Jenni promised that her hostess should have first refusal of any items she might come across in the course of her business.

'If all your clients are like that, I think I'd enjoy this work,' Jenni told Clay. They had stopped for a cup of tea at a motorway café on the way back to Southport.

'I must admit the Ramseys are a rather unique couple,' Clay said. 'But does that mean you've decided to come in with us?'

'I think so. But I want to talk to Phyl and Sonia first.'

'Fair enough,' Clay agreed. Then, 'While you and Freda were enthusing over her papier mâché, Joe was showing me his collection of maps. In fact I was able to tell him of some rather rare items coming up for sale next week down in London. He can't get away himself but he's asked me to bid on his behalf. It will mean staying away a couple of nights. Would you like to come?' He looked at her steadily and, Jenni felt, with underlying meaning.

## CHAPTER SEVEN

'WOULD you like to come with me, Jenni?' Clay repeated and though she knew she was blushing she did not avoid his gaze.

'Yes,' she told him simply. Her grey eyes, large and luminous, gave him the answer she could not put into words.

They drove down to London.

'If I do get hold of any of those maps,' Clay had told Jenni, 'I want to bring them back myself. I wouldn't like to trust them to any delivery firm.'

Clay was late picking her up and for the first part of their long journey he seemed *distrait* and preoccupied. Jenni respected his reserve. Conversation wasn't essential; she was content just to be in his company. But it was obvious he had something weighing heavily on his mind and she wondered if the day would ever come when he would confide his troubles to her.

Even in the short while she'd known him she had formed the impression of a man who was not entirely happy. When he laughed, which was rarely, he seemed to retain some of the grave remoteness of a man who had suffered or who suffered still. The thought that she might be the instrument of bringing him happiness was accompanied by an inner spasm of feeling that was part compassionate, part sexual in its origins.

Clay had booked them into a large hotel only a short distance from the auction-rooms. And though Jenni, certain now of her love for him, had made up her mind to do whatever he asked of her, it was a relief to find he had booked separate rooms. It meant he wasn't taking her acquiescence for granted.

In the end they had decided to stay away for three nights, travelling down the day before the viewing.

'So that gives us a night on the town if you like,' Clay suggested. 'We might take in a show, have a meal?'

He chose a small, intimate restaurant. Tonight he was more talkative but there was no mention of business. His every word, his every glance was a subtle wooing of her senses, and if anyone had asked her afterwards Jenni would have been unable to recall what she had eaten.

'Glad you came to London with me?' he asked, his hand covering hers where it rested on the table. Even his long spatulate fingers held a measure of his strong sensuality.

'Very glad.'

'So am I—and relieved. I was afraid that when it came to it you would refuse. Jenni,' there was a gravity in his blue eyes that subtly disturbed her, 'let's make the most of these few days, hmm?'

Jenni's heart lurched. It was almost as if he didn't expect many more opportunities for them to be together. She wished, not for the first time, that she knew the reason for his fits of depression. Surely he wasn't suffering from some incurable illness? There were those mysterious trips abroad. Could they be for health reasons? Anxiously, she scrutinised his blunt-featured face. He looked perfectly well, and yet you never knew.

Don't be ridiculous, she tried to reassure herself. He would hardly be making plans for them to collaborate in business if he thought his time was limited.

'What are you thinking about?' Clay asked curiously.

'Only about what you said,' she told him, 'about making the most of our time.'

'And do you agree with me?' It was said intensely.

'Yes.' Jenni's voice was soft and throaty.

'You know what I mean—what I'm asking of you?'

'Yes,' she said again, her grey eyes fearless.

'Oh, Jenni, Jenni!' A muscle worked in his throat.

Small though the restaurant was it boasted a dance floor and Jenni had been hoping Clay would ask her to dance. The longing to be in his arms was pure agony. Involuntarily, her eyes strayed towards the couples already on the floor and Clay must have read her thoughts. He didn't ask her. He simply stood up and held out his hand.

The first time they had danced together his touch had been almost impersonal. He had not held her particularly near to him. Yet even then she had been moved by his vibrant sexuality. This time, from the moment his arms went about her, she knew he shared her need to be close. She could feel the heat of his skin, the very faint tremble in his body which awoke an answering agitation in her own.

He danced as beautifully as she remembered, moving with a lithe co-ordination. But when the tempo of the music changed to a slow, dreamy waltz-time, Clay seized the opportunity to hold her hard up against him and dancing became only a pretence, the muscular length of his legs and stomach against hers in an intimate intoxication. His hands at the base of her spine explored and caressed. His lips brushed her temple, traced the outer convolutions of her ear.

'Oh, Jenni, you're so lovely.' His words were a groan. 'Have you any idea just how much I want you?' He didn't give her a chance to reply but went on, 'The first time I saw you I had a feeling you would alter my life. But I never guessed how much. Jenni,' he said her name again, hesitantly this time, 'tell me if I'm wrong, but I believe you are a little in love with me.'

She couldn't have lied if she'd wanted to, so deeply was she caught in the toils of sensuality.

'I'm completely and utterly in love with you,' she told him with unmistakable sincerity, and she felt his body's immediate response to her words.

'Do you want to carry on dancing?' he asked huskily. 'Or go on anywhere? Or shall we go back to the hotel?'

'The hotel, please.' Her voice was unsteady.

It wasn't far but the journey could not pass quickly enough for Jenni and she knew Clay felt the same. Even though he had to concentrate on his driving he emanated an overpowering aura of sensuousness. And in the lift he held her closely, not speaking, but there was no need for words.

Jenni's hand was trembling so much she could not insert the key into the lock of her bedroom door and Clay had to take it from her. He had barely closed the door behind them when he took her in his arms. And at once his hands were at her hair, loosening the rich mahogany coil so that the tresses lay thick and heavy on her shoulders.

'I want to see you naked,' he murmured, 'with your glorious hair spread over your breasts. I want to bury my face in your hair, bury myself in you. Oh, dear lord! I want to forget everything but you.'

'Oh, Clay!' Her voice was as weak as her knees as he began to unbutton her blouse. She had never dreamed that love could be like this, so all-engulfing. Everything she was or had ever been paled to insignificance before this moment in Clay's arms.

He began to trail kisses down her neck, into the hollow of her throat, down to the curve of her breasts, his lips and his tongue doing intoxicating things to her.

'Undress me, Jenni,' he begged and he shuddered violently as her hands edged beneath his shirt, pulling it free of his waistband.

When their clothes were a crumpled heap on the floor, for a moment Clay held her away from him.

'Let me look at you,' he said huskily and she felt as though the delicate colour must be staining her whole body as his eyes unconcealedly worshipped her.

He was beautiful to look at too. Strong and powerfully muscled. Jenni drank in every inch of his powerful body, his torso as tanned as his face.

'However did you get an all-over tan like that at this time of year?' she marvelled.

'Abroad.' He said it curtly and Jenni felt some of the responsiveness go out of him. She knew at once that she had touched on that part of his life that he kept concealed from her, and cursed herself for endangering their mood.

Swiftly, she bent her head and pressed her lips against his clean, male-smelling chest, circling the male nipples with her tongue, feeling the strong pounding of his heart against her mouth. To her relief he took her in his arms again, his warm, hair-roughened skin against the bare flesh of her breasts.

He lifted her from the floor so that their faces were on a level. Her arms clasped about his neck, her lips opening willingly to his.

'I want you, my darling Jenni.' His voice was husky, its throb echoing that of his body. 'Jenni, is it all right? Because I don't think I could bear it if you made me stop now.'

'I don't want you to stop,' she reassured him, her lips and hands reinforcing her words.

He carried her over to the bed and lowered himself down beside her, kissing her with a fresh onslaught of passion. And though her surrender was willing, for an instant Jenni knew a moment of fear. It was the first time she had given herself to any man. But he was gentle as well as passionate, his fingers caressing her slowly but so seductively that fire overcame fear. He played with each nipple in turn, watching them harden in response, bending his head to take them softly between his lips.

His touch moved lower, exploring, seeking and finding the secret places of her femininity until at last he set off an explosive reaction within her and she plunged her hands into his hair, crying out as she arched her hips towards him, pulling his mouth down to hers. Then his body covered hers, possessing her. He plunged deeply and rhythmically, and there was nothing but an intense ecstasy of sensation followed by a sense of utter physical satisfaction.

Clay lay on his back with Jenni curled into the protective circle of his arm. She studied his profile in puzzled silence. His eyes were wide open, staring up at the ceiling, and his face was withdrawn into an expression of remote inscrutability. And yet she knew their lovemaking had pleased him. At the climactic moment he had let out a cry of pure joy and she had felt the dampness of his tears upon her face. A great tenderness possessed her.

'Clay?' she said diffidently. It was odd. She knew him well enough, loved him strongly enough to share the greatest intimacy known to man and woman. And yet she felt she did not know him sufficiently well to intrude into the deepest recesses of his mind. Knew that, if she did, he would retreat into that mood of gloom which occasionally possessed him.

He turned to look at her.

'You were a virgin,' he said wonderingly.

'Yes.' She was puzzled. 'I thought you knew that.'

'No.' He shook his head. 'I didn't know. I didn't think it was possible in these days for a woman to reach the age of twenty-five and still retain such innocence.'

'Would it have made any difference if you'd known?'

'I don't know. Oh, I don't know. I wanted you so much.' He rolled on to his side and stared into her eyes. 'Don't get me wrong, Jenni. I feel incredibly honoured, very moved, to know I'm the first man to take you. But I can't help feeling guilty too. You see, it doesn't change anything.'

He meant that he still didn't intend to marry her. Jenni had gone into this situation with her eyes wide open, she couldn't pretend he had deceived her, but she still felt a stab of pain. She suppressed it valiantly, even though tears smarted behind her eyes.

'I realise that.'

Clay reached out and caressed her cheek, and Jenni, love surging through her, turned her head so that her lips brushed his palm.

'You're incredible,' he said softly. 'Do you know that? Some girls would have used their virginity as a weapon, an instrument of blackmail. But you wouldn't, would you?' And as she shook her head, 'I love you, Jenni Wallis,' he told her. 'I mean to make you happy as far as it's in my power to do so. Will you still settle for that?'

She couldn't settle for any less, not now that she had known what it was like to be loved by him. She told him so, even though it meant ignoring the small inner voice that said he had it in his power to make her even happier, if only he would. And the lips that returned to hers swept away the sound of that tiny voice until she was aware only of him and of his renewed need of her.

'It was Charles I who set the vogue for hanging framed maps as a decoration,' Clay said next morning as they viewed the sale items. 'The earliest maps were drawn by monks, of course, on sheets of parchment. It took them weeks to illuminate just one map by hand.'

'Will you be bidding for all of these?' Jenni asked.

'No, just a few. I imagine a lot of them will go beyond even Joe Ramsey's well-filled purse.' Clay moved on to the next lot number and whistled soundlessly through his teeth. 'Now there's an interesting little collection! Joe would be mightily pleased if I could get my hands on those.' He pointed to half a dozen particularly fine maps. 'Unless I'm very much mistaken, they're the work of one of the most famous cartographers of all time.'

Maps had never formed a part of Jenni's stock in

trade, and she studied the items with interest while Clay continued to enthuse.

'This chap specialised in depicting land battles and sea fights. Look, it's alive with ships, dolphins and puffing heads symbolising the four winds. Yes, I'll definitely be bidding for those.'

Jenni turned her attention to the rest of the sale-room.

'And I'm going for those teapots—for my own collection,' she decided. Most of the items she acquired had to be resold, but occasionally there were things she could not bear to part with and these had formed the nucleus of a collection. 'How about you,' she asked Clay. 'Is there anything you fancy for yourself?'

'Oh, yes!' Clay said and his blue eyes shone wickedly so that she knew immediately what was coming but she still blushed. 'I fancy you!'

'In the middle of the afternoon!' She pretended to be shocked.

'Any time, anywhere,' he told her, and now he wasn't joking, and Jenni swallowed as desire shafted through her.

As a buying trip, the three days were eminently successful. As well as the maps for Joe Ramsey, Clay secured several other items which would fit into his scheme for the Kirkby Lonsdale house. And Jenni was inordinately pleased to acquire some very fine old lace comprising Victorian wedding veils and some exquisite examples of Honiton.

'It's all the rage now with fashion designers,' she told Clay. 'I have a customer in Southport who'll buy up everything I can get hold of.'

But if the days were satisfactory the nights were

even more so, when they made love, Jenni
discovering in herself a passionate abandon that
surprised her. Afterwards they slept in each other's
arms, unwilling to be apart even for a few
hours.

'I needn't have booked two rooms,' Clay observed
jokingly.

'I'm glad you did,' Jenni told him. 'I wouldn't have
liked you to take me for granted.'

'I hope you'll never have to accuse me of doing
that.' His expression was grave. 'I don't think I'll
ever cease to marvel at the wonder of finding you and
the incredible joy of making you mine.'

But both days and nights passed all too quickly,
and just before dawn on the morning of their
departure Clay woke Jenni and made love to her with
an even more feverish urgency than he had shown
before. Afterwards, in the lovely aftermath of ecstasy
as they lay in each other's arms, Jenni felt Clay's
chest rise and fall in a heavy sigh.

She felt more like weeping herself. This little time
apart from the world was over. This time tomorrow
they would be sleeping in their own beds. If only she
could find him beside her every morning.

But fiercely Jenni controlled her emotions. She
wasn't going to antagonise Clay by demanding more
than he was prepared to give. She had known the
ground rules before she had gone into this
relationship. Too late to repine. Even so, she
was a little curious about that gusty breath of
his.

'Why the great sigh?' she asked. She raised herself
on one elbow so that she could look down into his
face. She was shocked by the bleakness of the
expression he was not quick enough to hide. 'Clay?'

she said worriedly.

'Take no notice of me,' he told her. 'I warned you I could be a moody creature. Come on.' He rolled out of bed. 'Let's not get introspective. Come and join me in a shower?'

The novelty of the suggestion took Jenni's breath away and—perhaps as Clay had intended—banished her concern for him.

Showering together, soaping each other's bodies inevitably led to other things and before long they were back in bed, sharing another of those glorious periods of intimacy, the memory of which, Jenni learned, she might have to exist on for some time to come.

'It may be a while before I can get away again like this,' Clay told her.

'But . . . but I will be seeing you . . . soon?' she ventured to ask. She didn't want him to think she was attaching the strings he had forbidden.

'As soon as I can make it.' He turned to look at her, his face strained, the blue eyes hungry. 'Never doubt that I want to be with you, Jenni, as soon and as often as I can.'


'You look different lately, Jen,' Sonia told her cousin a day or two after her return to Southport. They were packing up the van in readiness for market.

'Different? In what way?'

Sonia chewed her bottom lip.

'If I tell you,' she sighed, 'you'll probably tell me to mind my own business.'

'I'm not that much of an ogre, am I?' Jenni was amused.

'No,' Sonia said soberly. 'You're an old softy, which is the main reason I'm worried about you.'

'Oh? Do I look ill or something?'

'Far from it. You've had a sort of glow about you ever since you came back from London.' She hesitated, then she asked bluntly, 'Jenni, did you sleep with Clay?'

Jenni didn't need to say anything. Her sudden heightened colour said it all and her cousin drew in a sharp breath.

'Has he asked you to marry him after all?'

'No. He . . .'

'Oh, Jenni!' Sonia's expression of concern deepened. 'Sometimes I feel hundreds of years older than you. How long have you known Clay? No time at all.'

'Long enough,' Jenni said defensively. 'Long enough to know that I love him. And it's not just a physical thing, Sonia. If it had been I wouldn't have . . .'

'Maybe,' her cousin conceded, 'but do you think he ever *will* ask you to marry him?'

'I know he won't,' Jenni said quietly, and her cousin's fair eyebrows rose in horror. 'Look, love, I know you mean well. But I am of age, and these days it's no great deal if people want to sleep together instead of getting married. It's done all the time.'

'True,' Sonia conceded, then, shrewdly, 'but is that what you want?'

'No,' Jenni sighed, but then, with quiet dignity, 'but I've given it a lot of careful thought and I've accepted the situation.' Then she abandoned dignity for deep sincerity. 'Oh, Sonia, I do love him so much. Don't you see, I *couldn't* say no and lose him. And don't say he'd have come round to my way of thinking because I know he wouldn't. He's not a boy.

He's mature, experienced. He's had one unhappy marriage. He won't change his mind.'

At the end of this speech both girls had tears in their eyes and Sonia hugged her cousin.

'I understand. Maybe in similar circumstances I'd do the same. I don't know. But,' worriedly, 'I hope nothing goes wrong. If you feel that strongly about him it could destroy you.'

'What could go wrong?' Jenni asked with more confidence than she felt. Wasn't it her own nightmare that some day Clay would tire of their relationship, make use of its openness to discard her?

'You've been taking precautions, I hope,' Sonia said as they drove away from the shop.

'Of course. You may think me all kinds of a fool,' Jenni sighed, 'but I'm not a reckless fool. And I wouldn't try to bind Clay to me by deliberately getting pregnant.'

'And yet you've always wanted children.'

'Yes.' And then, with an irritation of which later she was ashamed, 'for heaven's sake, Sonia, let's drop the subject.'

Sometimes Jenni could almost believe London had been a dream as she and her cousin fell back into the routine of shop, market and antique fairs. Clay telephoned her regularly and she could hear the desire in his voice, but as the days passed she longed to see him again in the flesh, to feel the physical reassurance of his love. It was only the briskness of business which kept her from brooding.

She had another clash with Ursula, this time bidding successfully against the other woman for some very old dolls. These were to go to another of Clay's wealthy clients who collected toys of every kind.

'If looks could have killed,' Jenni told Sonia, 'I'd be in the undertaker's parlour right now.' And though her cousin crowed with delight over Jenni's victory, Jenni herself still had a sense of unease where Ursula was concerned. The fat woman was reputed to have a mean and vindictive nature.

'How could she possibly harm you?' Sonia asked, not for the first time, when Jenni confessed her feelings.

'I don't know. Call it intuition if you like.'

'You're just depressed,' Sonia said shrewdly, 'because Clay's just cancelled your date.'

It was true, Clay had telephoned that morning, cancelling a date he had made only two days previously, and Jenni had done something she had promised herself she would never do and questioned him.

'Why, Clay? I haven't seen you for ages.'

'I know. But it can't be helped.' There was no warmth at all in his voice. 'I have to go away.'

'Business?' she asked hopefully. 'Perhaps I could . . .'

'No, not business,' he interrupted curtly. 'A personal matter.'

'How long will you be gone?'

'I've no idea.' He sounded irritated now. 'Look, Jenni, I . . .'

'I know! No questions, no strings, right? OK. I'll see you when you get back.' And she did something she had never done to anyone else. She put the receiver down. But only so that he shouldn't hear the sudden sobs that choked her voice. She needed the reassurance of his presence. She needed to know that he still loved and wanted her. She needed *him*, her anguished body cried out.

The telephone rang again after a few minutes. But by now Jenni was in control again.

'Serendipity Antiques,' she said in her normal cool but friendly manner, though it cost her an effort to do so.

'Jenni!' It was Clay. 'Don't hang up on me again,' he warned. 'At least not until you've heard what I have to say. OK?'

'All right,' she said stiffly.

'I'm equally disappointed that I can't see you.' He spoke huskily. 'If you only knew how I need you—right at this very moment. But I warned you how it would be. Jenni,' and now he was pleading, 'don't ask me for more than I can give. If you can't accept things the way they are we'll have to call the whole thing off—for your sake as well as mine.' His words filled her with horror.

'Oh, no, Clay! Please!' She wasn't far from tears again. 'I'm sorry. I know what we agreed. But it's very hard . . .'

'Don't you think it's hard for me too?' There was a rough edge to his voice. 'Don't you think I'd rather be with you than . . .' He broke off abruptly. Than with whom? Jenni wondered but dared not ask. 'Look, my dear, I'll be in touch again, just as soon as I can. Please be patient with me.' And, urgently, 'Please wait for me, Jenni!'

'Clay's been away for almost a month now,' Sonia told Jenni now, somewhat unnecessarily. Jenni could have told her cousin the length of time to the hour since she had last seen him. 'And all you've had are a few measly postcards. There he is apparently enjoying himself in Switzerland and you're here eating your heart out. You don't think he's got someone else—abroad? He does go away rather a lot.'

'Oh, Sonia,' Jenni groaned, 'don't put any more doubts into my mind. I'm going mad as it is, wondering why he's so secretive about those trips, why he clams up about personal things. It's not as if I don't understand about him not wanting to get married again. I've never nagged about that.'

'Even so,' Sonia declared, 'if Tim treated me like that I'd soon give him the elbow.'

'It's rather difficult to give someone the elbow, as you so elegantly put it,' Jenni said wryly, 'when you don't even know where to contact them.'

'So you are considering it?'

'No,' Jenni said wearily. 'You probably think I'm a fool, but I'm going to stick it out until I see him again. But then,' she said resolutely, 'I'm going to insist on the answers to a few questions.' She sighed and Sonia's heart ached for her. 'Trust should be a two-way thing. If he expects me to go on trusting him it's time he credited me with enough discretion to share his problems. Because he obviously does have problems.'

The days went by. Customers came and went, all of them interesting in their way. But perhaps none quite so memorable as the one who visited Serendipity one Tuesday afternoon.

Quite a lot of side-street shops in Southport observed a half-day on a Tuesday. Some even closed for the full day. But Serendipity was open every day except Sunday. However, Tuesday was normally a quiet day for the two girls. Jenni was in the flat catching up on some accounts. Her cousin was in charge of the shop.

'Jenni!' Sonia arrived in the flat, breathless from the break-neck stairs. 'I know you're busy, but can you spare the time to come and see this customer?'

'Of course.' Jenni never denied herself to any prospective buyer. 'Problems?' she asked.

'Not exactly. But she's a bit of a madam and apparently I'm not good enough to serve her. She asked particularly for you.'

'OK.' Jenni pushed the long list of figures aside with a little sigh of frustration. She didn't get much time for paperwork, and maths wasn't her strong suit. She would far rather be in the shop selling. But accounts had to be done and the VAT inspector was due in a day or two.

'She says,' Sonia dropped something of a bombshell, 'that Ursula sent her to us.'

Jenni looked at her cousin sharply. That didn't sound at all like Ursula Bond—passing up a sale in favour of a rival—and Jenni saw Sonia shared her suspicions. The unscrupulous one was up to something. She followed Sonia downstairs into the shop.

'How can I help you?' Jenni asked the woman.

'I want to look at some paintings.' She had a high, light voice and cold grey eyes. She seemed to be in her middle thirties as far as Jenni could judge and she was still extremely attractive in a blonde, brittle way.

Jenni sensed at once that she was likely to be capricious and difficult to please. But even an awkward customer meant trade.

'Had you anything particular in mind?' she asked pleasantly. She gestured around the shop. 'We have quite a nice selection at the moment.'

Some of the paintings hung on the walls. But there was not room for all of them. The remainder were neatly stacked against a rear partition.

'Show me what you have. Bring them over here to the daylight. I shan't know what I want until I see it.'

Stifling a sigh, Jenni beckoned to Sonia to help her and one by one they submitted the paintings for inspection, some of them in quite heavy ornate frames. The first few met with a disdainful look and a wave of rejection from a thin, scarlet-tipped hand.

'Old bag!' Sonia muttered as they retreated to the rear of the shop for about the twentieth time. 'I'll eat my hat if she buys anything. I've met her sort before.'

The two girls dragged yet another picture forward.

'Hmm, that one's passable—and that. Leave those two by me.'

This ceremony continued until the woman had seen every picture the shop had to offer. Finally half a dozen paintings, ironically the largest and heaviest, were grouped about the customer and Jenni's arms and back were aching. And still the woman seemed uncertain.

'If we have nothing you like,' Jenni suggested, 'it's possible a friend of mine may be able to help. But his business is in Preston.' She was beginning to feel, as Sonia had predicted, that their customer would finally depart empty-handed.

'You mean Clay Cunningham, of course,' the woman said with a hard little laugh. 'No, thanks, there's no way I'd put any business *his* way. But Ursula told me you two were in cahoots.'

'Oh?' Jenni enquired. 'How do you come to know Ursula?'

'We've had some dealings. I've sold her one or two pieces.'

And lost by it, I bet, Jenni thought, but for once she felt no concern for one of Ursula's victims. It didn't happen often, but Jenni had taken an instinctive dislike to this particular customer and she was suddenly anxious to be rid of her.

'Perhaps, if you'd give me some idea of your décor, I could help you decide if any of these paintings will be suitable.'

'That's the difficulty,' the woman said fretfully. 'So hard to tell without seeing them in situ. You'd better bring them to my house tomorrow.'

It would probably be a wasted exercise, Jenni thought. However, business was business and she agreed to the ungraciously worded request.

'So long as you realise I'd need a decision on the spot,' she stipulated. 'I couldn't possibly leave such a large, valuable proportion of my stock. And I can't make it tomorrow. It will have to be Friday.'

Sonia, who had been attending another customer, was quite perturbed when she learned of the arrangement.

'How do you know she's bona fide? I don't like the fact that she knows Ursula Bond. And she's picked out the most valuable paintings. I'm sure Ursula's up to something.'

'It's possible,' Jenni admitted. 'But not probable. And I can't let possibilities rule my life.'

Despite her cousin's forebodings, Jenni set off on Friday morning with the half-dozen pictures safely packed and stowed in the shop's van. It was a nice day for a drive, one of those freak spring-like days February sometimes produced. She was seeing Clay the following evening, the first time for ages, and she sang to herself as she took the dual carriageway north towards Preston.

Melinda Wagstaff, the customer, had given Jenni an address on the far side of Preston, an area known as Nog Tow. There was a lot of new development in the area but Jenni knew it was an older house she was looking for. The Beeches proved to be a large, rambling, half-timbered building. It had once been a farmhouse and still stood in its own grounds. But the land all around it had been sold off for building and the windows of the old house seemed to glitter disdainfully at its modern plebeian neighbours.

Melinda Wagstaff met Jenni at the door and made no offer to help as Jenni carried the pictures into a large rear drawing-room. The paintings already hanging in the drawing-room were fine examples of impressionist art and far superior to anything Jenni had brought with her. She couldn't think why the woman would want to replace those. Still, it was not her place to question, and though she might find it impossible to like her customer it didn't look as if there was anything wrong with Melinda Wagstaff's money.

The next three-quarters of an hour was one of the most exasperating Jenni had ever spent, and after a while she began to feel that even if the exercise resulted in a sale it was one she would most willingly have forgone.

At last a final selection of two had been made and Melinda Wagstaff submitted them to a critical appraisal.

'No, they're all useless,' she decided fretfully. 'You'd better take them away. I could murder a drink.' Then, to Jenni's amazement, for she had not been afforded much courtesy, 'Will you have one?'

'No, thanks, not when I'm driving. But I wouldn't mind a cup of tea or coffee.' It had been exhausting work hanging and rehanging paintings and Jenni had to stifle her chagrin as she reloaded the heavy pictures into the van then returned to the drawing-room. At least she might as well get a coffee out of her abortive trip, she thought grimly.

To her further surprise, when the coffee had been brought by a disgruntled-looking maidservant, Melinda Wagstaff actually invited Jenni to sit down. But then she proceeded to subject her to a long, curious, almost insolent inspection.

'So you're Clay's little friend,' she said at last.

Since she could scarcely be referring to Jenni's height, Jenni took the remark to be meant in a derogatory sense. And she disliked the woman's quite unexpected reference to her private affairs.

'We're business associates, yes,' she said repressively.

Melinda Wagstaff's smile was sarcastic.

'And that's not all, or so I hear.'

'I don't think that's any of your business.' Jenni put down her half-finished coffee and made to rise but the other woman put out a restraining hand, and for all her slight build she was surprisingly strong.

'Let's call it a friendly interest, shall we? And I do think it's time someone gave you a friendly warning.'

Somehow Jenni couldn't imagine this woman being anyone's friend. Her voice dripped honey but the words lacked that true ring of sincerity. Again she tried to rise but the other held her back.

'If you're planning to say something against Clay, I should remind you there are laws about slander,' Jenni said frostily.

'Ah, but we have no witnesses. And besides, the truth can't be slander. And no one knows the truth about Clay Cunningham better than I do.'

'Has Ursula Bond put you up to this, by any chance?' Jenni demanded.

'You and Clay shouldn't have upset Ursula, should you, my dear? If you hadn't she might not have begun to look around for a way to get her own back—and remembered my connection with him. She knew very little about Clay, but she was surprised and delighted when I was able to supply her with some very interesting information.'

'Which, of course, she suggested you pass on to me? Well, I'm not interested.' This time Jenni succeeded in gaining her feet. 'You got me here under false pretences. You had no intention of buying any paintings, not with those . . .' she pointed to the impressionist works '. . . hanging on your walls. I'm leaving.'

Swiftly, Melinda Wagstaff inserted herself between Jenni and the door and Jenni heard a key click in the lock.

'You're not going anywhere until you've listened to what I have to say. Frankly I don't give a tinker's cuss if you ruin your life, but I have a few little scores to settle with Clay myself. And I think you *might* show a little more interest when I tell you that I used to be married to him.'

# CHAPTER EIGHT

'*You* were married to Clay?' Jenni said it incredulously, and the woman bridled.

'There's no need to sound so surprised.' Complacently preening herself, 'He was very much in love with me.' And Jenni felt as though an iron hand were squeezing her heart when Melinda Wagstaff went on, 'And he still can't keep away, you know, even though we are divorced.' Her expression became reminiscent. 'The first few months were heaven—sheer heaven. Clay was a fantastic lover.' Slyly, 'Still is. But perhaps you already know that?'

Jenni couldn't help the colour that ran up under her olive skin.

'Ah, I see you do,' Melinda Wagstaff exclaimed. 'Don't look so concerned about me knowing, my dear. I'm not his wife any more, so I have no rights, and I'm resigned to the fact that there are other women in his life. He's very virile! Well, make the most of *your* little affair. It wouldn't last five minutes if only I'd agree to go back to him.'

'I don't believe you!' Jenni exclaimed, but her mouth had gone dry and her legs felt as if they might not continue to hold her up.

'Believe it or not, as you like,' Melinda shrugged. 'Why should I lie to you? It won't last anyway if his sisters ever get to hear about you.'

'His sisters?' They were the last people Jenni had

expected to hear the other woman cite in her remarks about Clay.

'Why do you think I left him? What newly married woman wants her husband's sisters living with them, always underfoot, always causing trouble? They ruined my marriage, and if you were ever fool enough to marry him they'd do the same for you. But he won't ask you . . . Ah, I see I've hit the nail on the head,' she exclaimed as Jenni's expressive face gave her away. 'You'd like to marry him but he hasn't asked you, has he? Well, of course he wouldn't, when he's always begging me to go back to him. But I've told him, there's no way I'll live under his roof with those two again. It's unnatural, if you ask me, his relationship with his sisters, especially the older of the two, his twin.' Melinda Wagstaff's expression became venomous. 'If you ask me, there's something almost incestuous about it.'

'Stop it!' Jenni's hands were clenched into fists at her side. 'Don't you dare make such a filthy suggestion! Clay would never . . .'

'Oh, no!' Melinda interrupted, 'You're quite right. *He* never would. I've always believed his appetites to be quite normal.' Smugly, 'Otherwise he wouldn't still visit me so regularly. But that doesn't mean *she* wouldn't like to . . . The times I've caught her in his arms!'

'Shut up! Shut up, you foul-mouthed woman!' Jenni was beside herself with disgust and Melinda Wagstaff flinched as she advanced on her. But Jenni had no intention of resorting to physical violence, or at least only enough to get her out of this woman's presence. She pushed Melinda aside and unlocked the door. On the threshold, she turned for a parting shot. 'And you can tell your friend Ursula her little plan hasn't succeeded.'

'It has nothing to do with Ursula,' the other began. 'I . . .'

'No?' Jenni was ironic. 'Well, anyway, I don't believe a word of what you've said about Clay—or about his sisters. It's my belief that if anyone ruined your marriage, you ruined it yourself.'

'Then why can't he keep away from me?' Melinda demanded triumphantly, and Jenni had no answer. She turned to leave. 'But I'll tell you one thing,' Melinda shouted after her, 'he'll always put those sisters of his before anyone else. And judging by this afternoon's performance you haven't a fighting bone in your body. They'll walk all over you!'

Jenni felt physically sick as she ran from Melinda Wagstaff's house, her heels clattering on the flagged floor. She leaped into the van, selected first gear with uncharacteristic noisiness and accelerated away down the drive.

In the road outside Melinda's gates, she braked sharply and bent over the steering-wheel, fighting back the waves of nausea that threatened to overwhelm her. When she felt a little steadier she slid from the van and leaned against its side taking in great gulps of air. The encounter with Clay's ex-wife, her claims that he wanted her back, and her sordid insinuations about his twin had shaken Jenni to the core. How much of it was lies, how much truth? Was any of it true?

She was just about to climb back into the driving-seat and recommence her journey when a car came round the bend ahead of her. It was indicating to turn in through the gates to Melinda Wagstaff's house but when the driver saw Jenni, he slowed and stopped.

'Jenni?' Clay's voice was harsh, accusatory, 'what are you doing here?'

It was true. He did visit his ex-wife.

'I could ask you the same thing!' she snapped.

He was out of the car. Leaving the engine running and the driver's door open, he strode towards her. His good-looking features were taut with anger as he grasped her upper arm.

'Why are you prying into my private life, Jenni? What do you hope to gain by it? We had an agreement, remember?'

'It seems to me it was a rather one-sided agreement!' Jenni was shaking again, her face white with misery. 'I have no secrets from you. But it seems you have a whole lot you're keeping from *me*.'

'Nothing that I'm ashamed of!' he retorted. 'Damn it!' He cast an irritated glance over his shoulder. A line of cars had formed, waiting to overtake, and his car, parked opposite to Jenni's van, was blocking the road. 'I'll have to move my car. Wait here!' he commanded her.

But Jenni had no intention of doing any such thing. The moment he was back in the driving-seat she leaped into her van. At first she drove far too fast for the winding roads, so anxious was she to put as much distance between herself and Clay. But when she realised he wasn't following—and his powerful car could easily have overtaken her—she slowed to a more moderate pace. Later she had no recollection of having passed over the familiar route home, so whirlingly tumultuous had her thoughts been.

'It's a wonder you got home without having an

accident!' Sonia said indignantly. 'How could Clay speak to you like that!'

'What a set of people you seem to have got yourself involved with,' was Phyllida Wallis's comment.

The two women had been startled and then deeply concerned when Jenni had returned white-faced, exhausted and almost in tears. And such was her state of mind—repulsion at Melinda's accusations followed by her encounter with Clay—that it wasn't long before they had the whole story out of her.

'I knew that Wagstaff woman was trouble!' Sonia exclaimed. 'It's hard to imagine Clay fancying someone like that. And to think she made you drive all that way with all those paintings—when she had no intention of buying. Why couldn't she have said what she wanted to say right here?'

'Probably because our friend Ursula talked her into making me suffer as much as possible—and because she didn't want any witnesses to what she had to say. You were around all the time when she came to the shop, remember?'

'You don't believe what she told you—about his twin sister?' Sonia said hesitantly.

'*No I do not!*' Jenni was emphatic. 'But . . .'

'He's never invited you to meet his sisters?' That was undeniable. 'Will you tell Clay what Melinda said?'

Again Jenni shook her head. 'Not about his sisters. I wouldn't insult him by letting him think I needed to hear him deny it.' She shuddered. 'The whole thing's too unspeakably foul. Anyway right now I'm not even sure I want to see him again.'

'Then you do believe what Melinda said about him wanting her back?' Phyllida put in.

'I don't know,' Jenni said miserably. 'I just don't know what to believe.'

'I suppose,' Phyllida said soberly, 'if you've been married to someone there must always be a pull back to them. You see lots of cases in the news about people remarrying—and not just celebrities.'

'All the same, Jen,' Sonia said, 'I think you ought to meet his sisters. I don't believe Melinda Wagstaff's dirt any more than you do,' she added hastily when it looked as though Jenni would make some angry reply, 'but all the same, his sisters might have had something to do with his marriage breaking up. In-laws can cause all kinds of trouble.'

'That's true,' Phyllida put in. 'But in any event you ought to hear their side of the story. I didn't meet this Melinda Wagstaff. But from the sound of her I wouldn't believe a word she said without concrete evidence.'

'How can I meet his sisters?' Jenni demanded exasperatedly. 'For a start I don't know where they live. Clay's been very careful to keep that quiet. His telephone number is ex-directory. And anyway it wouldn't improve our relationship much. He already thinks I've been prying.'

'A man who's so secretive must have something to hide,' Phyllida suggested. 'The whole thing seems very unsatisfactory to me. Perhaps you would be better just to finish with him.'

'Perhaps,' Jenni said but simply because she couldn't face any further discussion of the subject. Right at that moment she sincerely doubted that there would ever be anyone else for her. She was certain that constant, inevitable comparisons would spoil her for any other man. Besides, how could she ever contemplate giving herself to another man when she had known Clay's lovemaking?

'Yes,' Sonia agreed. 'I should put him right out of your mind. It may take a while, but then you'll find someone else. And next time, for goodness' sake get a ring on your finger before you sleep with him.'

Just as Phyllida Wallis was making a move to go home and the two girls were thinking of going to bed—though Jenni doubted if she would sleep—the telephone rang.

'You answer it,' she told Sonia. 'I don't feel like talking to anyone right now. If it's business say I'll call back tomorrow.' But she knew at once from the expression on her cousin's face that this was no business call.

'I'm not sure she wants to speak to you,' Sonia said. She put her hand over the mouthpiece. 'It's Clay,' she said superfluously. 'He wants to talk to you.'

'I . . . I can't speak to him right now.' Jenni's heart was thudding sickeningly in her breast and she was trembling in every limb.

'You'll have to speak to him some time, dear,' Phyllida said worriedly.

'I know, but not tonight. I just can't. I can't take any more today.'

Sonia relayed her message.

'He says if you don't talk to him he's going to keep ringing this number all night.'

'Then we'll leave the receiver off,' Jenni said wearily.

This reply obviously had the desired effect because after listening for a few moments, Sonia replaced the handset.

'He was hellishly annoyed,' she reported.

'Oh, dear!' Phyllida worried. 'I do hope he doesn't

turn up on the doorstep and make a scene. So
unpleasant. So embarrassing. Do you think I'd better
stay the night?'

Jenni shook her head.

'We'll be all right, Auntie. Don't worry.'

The next morning passed in a blur of misery. Despite
her own late night a still concerned Phyllida arrived
early at the shop for her Saturday stint, suggesting
that Jenni take the day off.

'I'm sure Sonia could manage the market stall on
her own, or you could give it a miss for once.'

But despite her sleepless night and her depression,
Jenni shook her head. Work was the best antidote for
what ailed her.

'No, if we did that we might lose our spec. There
are always people ready and waiting to jump into a
vacancy. Besides if I sit around and think about
things I'll only feel worse.'

'Suppose Clay comes into the shop?' Phyllida
asked. 'Am I to tell him where you are?'

'He'll guess anyway, as it's market day.'

'So suppose he turns up at Ormskirk, then?' Sonia
asked as Jenni drove out across the flat area of land
known locally as 'The Moss.'

The van jerked slightly, then ran on smoothly once
more.

'I hope he won't,' Jenni said with a ragged edge to
her voice. 'I can't face him yet. But in any case he
can't say much in front of dozens of shoppers and
stallholders. I mean he can't *make* me talk to him, can
he?' It was a plea for reassurance but Sonia was
disconcertingly quiet.

'Are you sure you don't mind being left alone?' Clay

had not shown up at Ormskirk but Sonia had a date that evening. 'I could put Timothy off, say I had a hard day at the market.'

'No, you mustn't do that,' Jenni insisted. And as her cousin still looked doubtful, 'I'm not going to stick my head in the gas oven, you know!'

'You'd have a job,' her cousin muttered, 'we're all electric. No, but seriously, Jen . . .'

'Seriously,' Jenni said, 'I'll be all right.'

'But suppose Clay turns up tonight? Aren't you afraid?'

'I'm not afraid of Clay, Sonia.' And she wasn't—only of her reactions to him. 'Anyway, I'm ready to face him now. And I can't go on in this state of uncertainty forever. I need to know where I stand. I didn't sleep a wink last night and it was my own fault. I should have spoken to him when he phoned, but I couldn't trust myself.'

Phyllida too had to be discouraged from spending the evening with her great-niece. But in fact Jenni felt she would be glad of a few hours on her own. Without Sonia's anxious eyes constantly on her she would not have to keep up a cheerful front. She decided she would wash her hair and have a long soak in a hot bath, her sovereign remedy on the rare occasions in the past when her spirits had been low.

It didn't seem worth dressing again. So, in nightdress and dressing-gown she curled up in a deep armchair with a best-selling book she had been meaning to read for a long time. But somehow she couldn't get into the story. So-called best-sellers, she had discovered before, weren't always her cup of tea. Many of them she found pretentious. Clay had agreed with her. Clay . . . Perhaps it was the tedium of the book or perhaps it was the warmth from the bath but she slipped into a restless doze punctuated by dreams in which Clay figured but always as a mysterious, shadowy figure, frustratingly out of reach.

She woke with a start. The doorbell! She looked at her watch. Damn! Phyllida back again probably, egged on by Sonia who had still had grave doubts about leaving her alone.

'Hold on! I'm coming!' she cried as the doorbell let out another long shrill sound.

It was Clay. Tall, grave-eyed and unsmiling. He was dressed in cream-coloured trousers with a bright blue crew-neck sweater over a shirt. He looked incredibly, heart-turningly attractive.

'I hope you're not going to be difficult!' he said immediately and before Jenni's parted lips could utter his name. 'Because I warn you I'm not going away.'

She had pictured this moment a dozen times, rehearsing it. How she would behave, what she would say? But at the sight of him, his face so familiar, so dear, all preconceived ideas fled away.

'You . . . you'd better come in.' She led the way back to the living-room and sank down into the chair she had occupied before his arrival. But Clay ignored the seat she indicated. Instead he paced restlessly about the room, picking up an ornament here, straightening a picture there.

'Why did you refuse to speak to me last night?' he demanded.

'I . . . I wanted time to think,' Jenni said in a low voice.

'However long you took to think,' he retorted, 'you

couldn't come up with a motive I'd accept for your going behind my back to Melinda.'

'I did not go behind your back!' she cried indignantly. 'It was pure coincidence. I . . .'

'Pull the other one!' He slammed down a valuable vase with such ferocity that Jenni feared it would crack. 'It's got bells on! I don't believe in coincidence.'

'All right. Maybe it wasn't a coincidence!'

'Then why lie about it?'

'I'm not lying. And I haven't been prying into your private affairs. If you'd just listen for a moment instead of prowling round like a lion about to spring on its prey . . . I had no idea when I went to Melinda Wagstaff's house that she was your ex-wife. She came here, to the shop, looking at paintings. She said she wanted to see some in situ. So I . . .'

'And how did she very conveniently pick on *your* shop?' He came to a halt before her chair.

'Ursula Bond recommended . . .'

'Ursula Bond recommended a customer to go to a rival!' He laughed disbelievingly.

'I know. I thought the same. That's why . . .'

'Besides, how the hell would Melinda know her?'

'She said she'd sold some things to Ursula.'

Clay stared at her then swore vehemently.

'Now that I *can* believe!' He began to pace again. 'Hasn't she had enough money out of me without selling off the things I worked hard to acquire?'

Jenni looked blank. 'I don't understand.'

'I pay her alimony—and believe me, it's not peanuts. But we're still in dispute about the house and the contents. The case has been dragging on for the last year and meanwhile I can't touch a thing. But she, it seems, has been raising money on the contents.'

'That was your house? But she said *she* left *you*. She said . . .' At the memory of some of the things Melinda had said Jenni's voice faltered.

'Oh? And what other lies has my dear ex-wife been telling you?' And as Jenni made no answer he leaned over her and grasped her wrist, the sensation sending a tingling sensation through her whole body. 'Come on! Obviously there was more, or you wouldn't be looking so uncomfortable.'

'L . . . let go!' Panicked by his usual devastating effect upon her she tried to struggle free but he was too strong for her.

'*Tell* me, Jenni!'

'She . . . she said you . . . you still wanted her back.'

'She what?'

'She said that you . . . that you and she . . .'

'Go on!' Clay wasn't letting her off the hook.

'That you . . . you still went there to . . . to make love to her,' Jenni said in a low voice, unable to meet the penetrating stare of those blue eyes.

'And did you believe her?' His tone was ominous and now his hold of her was painful.

'I . . . I didn't know what to believe. And then, when you turned up on her doorstep . . . Clay, you're hurting me.' But he ignored her protest.

'You *did* believe her!'

'Well, what was I supposed to think? After all, I haven't known you that long. You only see me when it suits you. Clay, I'm beginning to think I made a mistake. I don't think we should go on.'

'Don't say that! Don't ever say that!' His voice was harsh, angry, and now he was gripping her by both shoulders, pulling her to her feet. 'Jenni, for pity's sake don't let us lose what we have because of that stupid woman's lies.' He pulled her up into his arms. 'You're so beautiful, Jenni, you have such tranquillity. You've brought a peace into my life that I'd forgotten existed.'

His power and virility, communicated through the touch of his hands, was bringing back to her all the moments they had spent together. But she didn't want to dwell on the hours she had lain in his arms, the ecstasy that had been theirs. She tried to free herself but without success.

'Let's get this quite straight.' Her voice was unsteady. 'Are you saying you want me to go on being . . . being your mistress? Because that's what I am, isn't it? I thought I could live with that, but I wasn't prepared to share you. Melinda might be, but . . .'

'Melinda has no share in me!' Clay said fiercely. 'Get that through your head. And even though I can't offer you marriage, I love you, I want you. I can't go back to living in a desert. No love. No woman in my bed to take and give the passion I need. And if words can't convince you, let's see if this will.'

With a fierce jerk he pulled her closer and she felt the tautness of his body against hers. His hands moulded their way along her figure, welding her to him, his hard arousal an erotic demand. His mouth sought hers, a hungry invasion, brooking no denial, bruising her lips apart.

And as, despite herself, she began to respond, his kiss became a coaxing caress and her body remembered how it felt to have his nakedness against hers, recalled the magnetic chemistry of his seeking hands, his utter possession of her, the sweet intimacy of mind and body they had shared.

Her weakness transmitting itself to him, his hands began to move gently, expertly, tenderly insistent, sensually arousing, and Jenni felt desire grow and expand until her response was more than submission, became a demand as strong as his own. With her hands she shaped his head, winding her fingers into the luxuriant thickness of the greying blond hair.

'How can you believe there is anyone else for me?' he muttered. 'And it's not just sex.' His voice became softer, huskier. 'You know our love goes deeper than the physical, Jenni. *Doesn't it*?'

'Yes. Oh, yes, Clay,' she said weakly.

The pressure of his body grew in intensity, fuelling her need, and with a sudden hoarse cry he swung her up into his arms, and moving with her towards the bedroom door, set her down tenderly on the bed.

'I'm going to make love to you, Jenni, as we've never made love before.'

Perhaps if he hadn't spoken, hadn't broken the spell he had woven about her, he might have succeeded in his intention.

'No, Clay.' Jenni sat up and scrambled off the other side of the bed. 'I'm sorry. But I can't just go on the way we were before. I thought I could, but I can't. I suppose I was wrong to agree in the first place. It's not enough. Clay, it has to be all or nothing.'

He stood transfixed, his hand still at the buttons of his shirt.

'By "all" you mean marriage?'

'Yes. If you're telling me the truth about Melinda—and you really do love me, I can't see any good reason why.'

'Can't you?' he said savagely. 'Well, I can.' He sat down heavily on the edge of the bed. 'For one thing—all other considerations apart—I can't afford to get married. And,' as Jenni parted her lips to speak, 'don't you dare tell me you have enough money for both of us.'

'I wasn't going to. I . . .'

'Good. Because there is no way in this world I'm going to live off a woman.' He drew a steadying breath and went on more calmly. 'Once, I was a reasonably prosperous man. I swore I wasn't going to live a hand-to-mouth existence as my parents did—as we did when we were kids. I worked, I studied and I sweated to get where I was. I had a house, a decent income. Enough for my needs and then . . .'

'And then?' Jenni queried.

'And then—among other things—I met Melinda. And for various reasons which I won't go into our marriage didn't work out.'

'I think you'll have to go into them,' Jenni told him. 'Because, you see, Melinda made certain allegations and I'd rather like to hear your side of the story.'

'Damn it! How can I tell you my version if I don't know what she said?'

'She talked about your sisters.'

'I see.' He was tight-lipped. 'And just what did she say about Clare and Georgie?'

'That they were the cause of your marriage breaking up. That you always put them before her.'

'Is that all?' And as Jenni hesitated—only momentarily, but visibly, 'Is that all, I said?'

'No,' she admitted uncomfortably. 'But the rest doesn't matter. It . . .'

'It matters to me. It's my sisters we're talking about. I want to know just what lies Melinda has been telling. And, Jenni, I'm going to sit here until you tell me,' he threatened.

She told him.

For a moment she thought he hadn't taken in what she said. He was so still—as if made of stone. Then he rose to his feet and stood looking down at her and the expression of loathing and disgust on his face made her shiver even though it couldn't be for her. But, incredibly, it was.

'And you believed that too, didn't you? *Didn't you?*' he shouted.

'No!' Jenni gasped. If she had thought for one moment he would think that, wild horses wouldn't have dragged the tale from her.

'Yes, you did. Otherwise why would you suddenly be so anxious to be rid of me? No one in their right mind could believe I wanted Melinda back. But *you*, you could believe that about my sister! *My sister!*' he repeated in anguished tones. 'If only you knew!'

'Clay!' Jenni came round the bed towards him, her hands outstretched. 'Clay, I didn't believe it, not for a moment. I would never have mentioned it if you hadn't insisted.' But he didn't appear to be listening.

'There comes a time in everyone's life, Jenni, when they have to make a decision. I've had to choose before between my own needs and those of my family, so it won't come so hard this time.'

'Clay?' she cried desperately. 'What are you saying?'

'I'm saying that there's no need for you to send me away. I'm going. I've never struck a woman in my life but you'll never know how close I came to it just now. That I should live to hear such filth on your lips, lips I've kissed . . .' He made a gesture of repulsion and turned on his heel.

It wasn't fair. He had *made* her repeat Melinda's lies. Jenni stumbled after him, her eyes blinded by tears, missed her footing over a scatter rug and measured her length on the floor. By the time, bruised and winded, she had regained her feet, Clay was gone and only the echoes of a slammed door proved that he had ever been there.

# CHAPTER NINE

'GOSH, Jen, you've got guts.' Sonia's voice was filled with sympathetic admiration. Worried about her cousin, she had returned earlier than usual, to find her fears justified and Jenni in a state of stunned misery. 'I don't think I would have dared to tell Clay about Melinda's allegations. Was he very angry?'

'That's putting it mildly.' Jenni gave a little hiccuping sob. She couldn't bear to think of how much Clay must hate her now.

'Clay? Hate you? Never!' Sonia said when her cousin voiced this thought. 'When he's had time to think about it he'll realise how unfair it was to turn on you like that. If he doesn't, he's not the man I thought him and you're well rid of him. But I bet you haven't seen the last of him.'

But at first it seemed that she had. For a while Jenni went to market, to auctions and fairs in fluttering anticipation of an encounter. But as the weeks dragged by there was no sign of Clay at any of the places they might have expected to meet and now she ached to see him, to have a chance to put the record straight. Surely by now his temper must have cooled. And then, one Thursday . . .

'Jen!'

It was about five o'clock in the morning when Sonia woke her cousin.

'Jen!' she croaked again. 'I'm sorry to be a nuisance

at this ungodly hour of the morning. But I thought you ought to know, I feel dreadful. I think I've got flu or something.'

Jenni switched on the bedside light and looked at her cousin. She did indeed look dreadful.

'Back to bed!' she ordered. 'And I'll bring you some aspirin and a hot drink.'

'This would have to happen on market day, just when you need me most,' Sonia said as Jenni tucked her in.

'I'll manage.'

'Look,' her cousin suggested, 'let me give Timothy a ring. I'm sure he'll give you a hand unloading and packing up again at the end of the day.'

Timothy proved quite willing to oblige and Jenni set off. Phyllida Wallis would be in the shop all day, so she had no anxiety about leaving Sonia. Her great-aunt would have no hesitation in telephoning for the doctor if it seemed necessary.

March had come in like a lamb but it was going out like a lion. The winds were blowing icily around the little market town and Jenni's stall was in a particularly vulnerable position, on the corner by the clock tower—once the site of the old village cross. But the weather didn't seem to deter the shoppers and she was kept continually busy. She and Timothy took it in turns to keep an eye on each other's stalls during very necessary coffee breaks.

'It's been a good day's trading,' Jenni said to Timothy in an all-too-brief slack period towards mid-afternoon. 'If it hadn't I think I'd have been glad to change places with Sonia—in a nice warm bed with Aunt Phyl fussing round me.'

Timothy came round behind her stall.

'Talking of Sonia,' he said, 'you're her cousin and

you seem to be good friends too. I expect she tells you most things. Do you think she really likes me?'

'I'm sure she does.' Jenni was surprised by the gravity of his question.

'You see,' Timothy went on earnestly, 'I'm very fond of her—very fond indeed, but she's just a kid really. I'm quite a bit older and I'm not sure how seriously she takes me.' He put a hand on Jenni's arm. 'Jenni, what do you think of this? I'd value your expert opinion.' He held out a little antique ring for her inspection.

'It's beautiful,' Jenni told him sincerely. 'It's quite a valuable one too.'

'It was my grandmother's. She left it to me. I've always hoped the girl I marry would wear it. Do you think it would fit Sonia?'

'I can soon tell you. Our fingers are the same size.'

Timothy slipped the ring on to Jenni's engagement finger. It was a perfect fit and she turned the hand from side to side admiring the ring as the many-faceted stones caught the light.

'Do you think she'd have me?' he asked wistfully.

About to tell him she couldn't speak for Sonia in that respect, Jenni's words were strangled at birth by an unlooked-for interruption. Intent on Timothy's confidences, she hadn't seen anyone approach the stall.

'You didn't waste much time finding yourself a new boyfriend, did you?—and a fiancé to boot, it seems!'

Jenni swung round, the blood draining from her cheeks.

'Clay!' His handsome face swam before her eyes.

He interpreted her exclamation as one of dismay.

'Oh, carry on! Don't mind me. I suppose it's what I deserve for giving in to my foolish need to see you again.' And before she could gather her wits he had turned on his heel and disappeared once more into the milling crowds.

'What the blazes was all that about?' a puzzled Timothy asked.

Jenni's first impulse was to run after Clay, to make him listen, to explain. But second thoughts and pride prevailed. Clay would be hurt and angry to think she had apparently got over him so soon. But it was his own fault for jumping to conclusions—again.

She removed the ring and handed it back to Timothy.

'Just a misunderstanding,' she told him in a voice that croaked, then, 'I should ask Sonia to marry you the next time you see her if I were you. And I wish you luck . . .' bitterly, 'more luck than I seem to have in my love-life.'

Light had dawned on Timothy.

'Oh, was that the fellow Sonia told me about? 'nough said.'

Jenni put on a brave face for the rest of the day but that night, in the privacy of her room, she shed scorching tears. It really hurt to know how shallow and fickle Clay must be thinking her.

'You'll be ill next,' Sonia told her a few days later when Jenni was still obviously moping. 'I know it's easy to say but maybe you should start socialising again, really find someone else.'

Jenni shook her head. No one could ever take Clay's place.

She had always been dedicated to her work. But

now she threw herself into it with even more single-mindedness.

An adjacent property had become vacant and she had been thinking seriously about extending Serendipity. And then Timothy put a proposition to her.

'Sonia and I are getting married in October. Is there any chance of you taking us in as partners? We will be sort of related and I'd be prepared to make a capital investment.'

'You can come in with me right away if you like,' she told him. 'As you say, we'll be related by marriage. Serendipity has always been a family business and, as I don't look like having any descendants . . .'

'Oh, come off it, Jenni,' said Timothy uncomfortably. 'Things may work out for you yet. You're young and far too attractive to live the rest of your life like a nun. I still feel guilty about that day at Ormskirk. I sometimes think I ought to look Cunningham up and tell him things weren't what they seemed.'

Although Jenni was pleased to be going into partnership with Sonia and Timothy it was a bitter reminder of the time when she had contemplated a similar arrangement with Clay. It was fortunate, she reflected, that nothing formal had been drawn up. The necessary process of dissolving their partnership could have been long and painful.

She was reminded again of their intended association when one Saturday morning—out of the blue—Joe and Freda Ramsey, Clay's clients from Kirkby Lonsdale, walked into the shop.

'Hello, Jenni, my dear,' Freda Ramsey said. 'We're in Southport for an autumn break and we remembered you had a shop here.'

'We thought we'd look in,' Joe contributed, 'renew our acquaintance and see if you had anything in our line.'

But as the Ramseys browsed around the shop it soon became evident that buying antiques wasn't all they had in mind.

'Are you still in partnership with Clay Cunningham?' Freda asked as she inspected a piece of papier mâché she fancied for her collection.

Jenni bit her lip.

'No,' she said. 'It . . . it didn't work out. I'm going into partnership with my cousin and her future husband instead.'

'That's a pity.' Joe had wandered over to join in the conversation. 'We were hoping you might be able to put us in touch with Cunningham. We've lost track of him.'

'Lost track of him?' Jenni's hands had begun to shake so much she had to put down the piece of porcelain she was dusting.

'All we had was a telephone number, of course,' Joe told her. 'But every time we've rung just recently there's been the discontinued signal. Just in case it was a fault, we checked with the telephone exchange and it's quite right. There's no one at that number any more.'

'I'm sorry,' Jenni said slowly, 'but I'm afraid I can't help. I . . . I don't see him any more.' Her heart was pounding heavily in her chest and nausea threatened her. Where had Clay gone?

After making a few purchases the Ramseys left, promising to call in again next time they were in the area.

Jenni said nothing of this conversation to her

cousin. She knew Sonia would only worry about her intended course of action. She had a delivery to make next day in the general direction of Preston—she often made deliveries on a Sunday, her only free day. She had decided to pay a visit to Deborah and Nobby Clarke.

It was a beautiful day. Spring seemed to have arrived and the road from Southport to Preston was clogged with traffic making its way to Blackpool. After a frustratingly slow journey, Jenni made her delivery first and then, with her heart pounding in her throat, she drove on along the country lanes.

'Miss Wallis! Jenni!' Nobby Clarke opened the front door to her. 'How nice to see you again.' After Clay's initial introduction of her as a prospective partner Jenni had not met the Clarkes again. 'Come in.' He led the way into the drawing-room. 'Look who's here, Deb. What can we do for you, Jenni?'

'You can tell me where I can find Clay,' she said without preamble.

Nobby threw a doubtful glance at Deborah, who answered for him.

'If you don't have Clay's address,' she said slowly, 'then you're not as close to him as we supposed. I really don't think we can help you.'

'Oh please!' Jenni was suddenly in tears. 'We are close . . . We *were*,' she corrected. 'B . . . but there have been a couple of dreadful misunderstandings. And Clay was so angry he didn't give me a chance to explain.' It wasn't easy to plead like this with Deborah Clarke. Jenni had never been quite sure that she liked the other woman.

'Hrrmph!' Nobby, a man obviously made

uncomfortable by female tears, edged towards the door. 'Better tell Deb all about it, my dear. Let her be the judge. Good friends, Deb and Clay. Tells her things.' Abruptly he vanished.

Deborah laughed ruefully.

'Poor old Nobby! He's one of the stiff-upper-lip brigade. He'd never bare his soul to a woman the way Clay did to me.' And Jenni felt a sharp pang of envy. If only Clay had seen fit to trust *her* with his problems. She felt sure she could have offered him as much in the way of sympathy and support. 'But Nobby's right,' Deborah continued. 'I'd have to be sure your motives were right before I could tell you anything about his private life.' She looked at Jenni, perhaps seeing the reluctance in her face, for she went on in a kinder tone of voice. 'I suspect that you have mixed feelings about me. Our first encounter was rather unfortunate. But if you can bring yourself to confide in me I promise it shan't go beyond these four walls. Think about it, while I make us a cup of coffee.'

By the time Deborah Clarke returned from the kitchen Jenni had made up her mind. This was no time for pride or embarrassment. It could be her only chance of winning back Clay's affection. She had to take it.

Deborah listened in silence while Jenni related the facts of her growing friendship with Clay, their short but passionate closer relationship, the encounter with Melinda. Only once did Jenni's voice falter as she spoke of Melinda's unpleasant insinuations about Clay's twin. And only then did Deborah break her silence, drawing in a sharp breath, her mouth compressing into angry lines.

When Jenni had finished, Deborah sat quietly for a

moment. Hands clenched in her lap, her lips trembling, Jenni waited for her verdict. At last Deborah seemed to come to a decision, for with a decided little nod of her head she rose to her feet.

'I happen to know that Clay's away at the moment. I can tell you where to find him, but first I'd like you to come somewhere with me.'

As Jenni followed her into the hallway, her heart beating with nervous anticipation, Deborah put her head round another door, calling to her husband that she was going out.

'Nobby's study—his retreat,' she told Jenni smilingly. 'When anything threatens to get too emotional for him he disappears in there.'

Deborah made absolutely no explanation of where they were going and now that she felt some help was being offered Jenni was content to await events. They drove from the Clarkes' house on the outskirts of Preston into some of the town's meaner-looking streets until finally Deborah pulled up outside a row of terraced houses. Jenni knew Clay wasn't well off but she hadn't expected quite this setting.

'Clay and his sisters have been renting this place while he's in dispute with Melinda over the Beeches.' She turned in her seat to look at Jenni. 'I must beg you not to repeat anything of what you told me to Clare and Georgie.'

'Of course not!' Jenni promised willingly.

'Deborah! How lovely to see you. And you've brought us a visitor!' The girl who answered the door was tall and slender. She had Clay's vivid blue eyes and her shoulder-length hair was the golden colour his must once have been before the years had faded it. She couldn't be more than eighteen or nineteen,

Jenni decided.

'I hope it's not inconvenient,' Deborah said anxiously. 'I couldn't telephone ahead and ask. Your phone seems to be out of order.'

'It was cut off about a month ago,' the girl grimaced. Then, 'Jenni, this is Clay's younger sister, Georgie. Georgie, this is Jenni Wallis, a friend of Clay's.'

The front door opened straight into the living-room. As the three women sat down Georgie looked at Jenni with eager intentness.

'Oh, I am glad Clay has a girlfriend. We were afraid the awful Melinda would have put him off women for life. But you look nice. Is she nice, Deb?' she asked the older woman artlessly.

'I think so,' Deborah replied with a smile. 'And I believe your brother thinks so too. Look, Georgie, I have some shopping to do while I'm in Preston. Suppose I leave you and Jenni to get acquainted? And perhaps Clare might feel up to having a visitor.'

There was a few moments' bustle as Deborah departed and Georgie insisted on offering her guest a cup of coffee which, having recently had one with Deborah, Jenni could well have done without. Then there was silence as the two girls sipped their drinks and took stock of each other. Without Deborah's presence, Georgie seemed suddenly shy. She gave a little laugh.

'Well, where do we start?'

'Tell me about yourself,' Jenni suggested, 'and your sister. She's Clay's twin, isn't she?'

'Yes.' All the glow went out of Georgie's mobile face and the blue eyes were sad. 'Poor old Clare. She leads a pretty dismal existence. It'll be nice for her to see a new face. I'll take you up in a minute.'

'I gather she's been ill,' said Jenni.

'It's not so much a case of *been* ill as *is* ill,' Georgie
sighed. 'She has one of these awful illnesses that
there's no known cure for. She's just wasting away
before our eyes. Clay's tried everything. He's spent a
fortune on private medicine, trips to Swiss
sanatoriums. He even took her to America once to see
some specialist. But it's no use.'

Jenni was horrified.

'You mean she's going to . . .' She couldn't say the
word.

Georgie's eyes were swimming with tears.

'I'm afraid so. But in the meantime she just drags
out an existence in that bedroom upstairs. When
Clay's around he carries her down here and he takes
her out in the car whenever he can.'

'How long has she been ill?'

'About two years. Oh, it's so unfair!' Georgie
jumped up and began to pace the room in a manner
that reminded Jenni irresistibly of her brother. 'Until
then her life was so interesting. She was an air
hostess. She travelled all over the world. Her
husband was a pilot with the same line.'

'Was?' Jenni queried sensing further tragedy.

'Yes. Was.' Georgie's young face became scornful.
'He couldn't take Clare's illness. Lord knows
whatever happened to "in sickness and in health".
He just upped and left her. If she hadn't had Clay to
turn to . . .' Georgie shrugged expressively.

'And you,' Jenni said gently.

'Yes, I was living at home at the time.' She
wrinkled her nose, a shorter, even more retroussé
version of Clay's. 'It wasn't all roses, believe me,
living under the same roof as the dreaded Melinda.

She and Clay had only been married a short while and she made it quite obvious she didn't like me being there. I was our parents' afterthought,' Georgie explained for Jenni's benefit. 'And when they died Clay promised he'd look after me. And he has.' Her face glowed with love for her brother. 'He insisted I go to university and I'm in my second year—I'm just home for a few days for Easter. I wanted to pack it in and get a job after Clay's divorce. Melinda milked him for every penny she could get. But Clay wouldn't hear of me leaving. I just don't know how he's managed this past year. Alimony, Clare's medical expenses and someone to look after her when he had to work, supporting me. He's been a real brick. He was quite well off until all this happened.'

It explained a lot that had puzzled Jenni. Clay's lack of wealth in spite of an obviously thriving partnership with the Clarkes, his sudden trips abroad, his constant urgent telephone calls home. Oh, if only he had seen fit to trust her with all this information.

'Can I meet Clare now?' she asked.

Georgie led the way into the communicating kitchen, the only other downstairs room, and up narrow, boxed-in stairs. A brief glance around showed Jenni that the upper floor boasted only two bedrooms and a small bathroom.

'This must have been a big change after living at the Beeches,' she commented.

'You've seen the Beeches?' Georgie exclaimed eagerly. 'How is the dear old place? Yes, it was a wrench, for all three of us. I hate the thought of Melinda living there amongst all Clay's lovely things. She's a *cow*!' she said vehemently. And then, 'I suppose if you've been to the house you must have met her.'

'Yes!' Jenni said. It was only one word but very expressive and Georgie giggled.

'You surely didn't go with Clay? The poor old boy has to go and see her every so often, with their solicitors. The negotiations about the house, you see? Melinda doesn't drive and she refuses to come into Preston.'

Georgie opened one of the bedroom doors and ushered Jenni in.

'Clare, isn't it fabulous, Clay's girlfriend's come to see us.'

'I didn't even know he had one,' a weak voice from the bed replied.

Jenni's heart turned over with pity as she stared into the wasted features, a travesty of Clay's own healthy face.

'Oh, you look like Clay,' she breathed.

'I'm surprised you can tell,' the other girl said wryly. 'I look such a sight these days I don't look in mirrors.' A limp hand lifted from the wrist. 'If you want to shake hands I'm afraid you'll have to do the shaking.'

Instead of shaking the emaciated hand Jenni sat down on the side of the bed and took it in both of her own.

'I'm so sorry about your illness,' she said. Always easily moved by the troubles of others, her grey eyes swam with tears. 'Do you have much pain?'

'Fortunately, no. I think that would be an unbearable addition. But let's not talk about my boring old illness. Tell me about you, how you met Clay. Are you going to marry him?'

Jenni related the details of her early encounters

with Clay, making humorously light of their battle over the oil paintings.

'But, no, I'm not going to marry him,' she concluded.

'Oh but why not? Don't you want to? Don't you love him?' Clare demanded, as if, Jenni thought, she couldn't visualise anyone not loving her twin.

'Oh, yes, I love him,' she said softly. 'But he doesn't want to get married again. I suppose that's Melinda's fault.'

'No!' Clare said savagely, and then, on a strangled sob, 'Oh, he should never have married her. But it's my fault.' It was agonising to see the tears streaming uncontrollably down the sick girl's face. She couldn't even lift a hand to wipe them away and it was Georgie who performed that office for her.

'I'm sorry,' Jenni herself was distressed. 'I shouldn't have come here, upsetting you. But I'm sure you're wrong.'

Surprisingly, it was Georgie who answered.

'No, she's right. But it's my fault too. We're both financial burdens on Clay. But he doesn't give a damn about that. What really got to him was the way Melinda treated us. She really resented us living with them. She tried to make our lives such hell that we'd leave. But we couldn't—Clare for obvious reasons and me because I simply couldn't afford to. Anyway, Clay wouldn't hear of it.'

'And I suppose Melinda was jealous,' Jenni suggested.

'Yes,' Georgie confirmed. 'Especially of Clare. Being twins, Clay and Clare have a special affinity. Clare gets awfully depressed sometimes and Melinda used to hate it when Clay tried to comfort her. She used to make awful snide remarks.'

Jenni could imagine.

'Anyway,' Georgie went on. 'Clay told me once that no one would ever hurt Clare and me that way again. That he was finished with marriage. I told him not to be so silly. But he said he wasn't going to risk bringing another woman to live under the same roof as us. That as far as he was concerned we came first. I told him not all women were like Melinda. Jenni, if you married Clay,' she asked ingenuously, 'you wouldn't want to throw us out, would you?'

'I most certainly would not,' Jenni told her. 'I was an only child and I always wanted to belong to a family. I'd have two ready-made sisters. But,' she said soberly, 'it isn't likely to happen. Clay and I aren't even on speaking terms.'

'Why not?' Georgie demanded.

'Georgie!' Clare was in command of herself once more and she spoke reproachfully. 'You don't ask people things like that.'

'Well, at least now he can't say he can't afford to get married,' Georgie said without any sign of contrition.

'How's that?' Jenni asked breathlessly. 'Has Melinda . . .?'

'That does look like being resolved,' Clare said, 'but there's more. Those oil paintings you spoke of.' Her thin pale face was irradiated for a moment and Jenni could see how lovely she must once have been. 'Clay heard just over a week ago that they'd been sold, in London, for a fantastic amount of money.'

'So they *were* Constables!' Jenni exclaimed.

'You're not still angry because you didn't get them?' Georgie asked anxiously.

'No. I got over that long ago. It would have been

nice to make a find like that, but Clay deserves it far more than I do. I suppose most people would say I'm very well off.'

'And that would be another reason Clay wouldn't ask you to marry him?' Clare asked. 'He's very proud.'

'But he will now, surely?' Georgie said.

'Not unless I can see him and sort out our differences,' Jenni told her sadly.

'Then you must go and see him—at once!' the impetuous Georgie insisted.

'I will—if you'll tell me where to find him.'

Speed restrictions had never seemed so frustrating as Jenni drove back to Southport and on towards Liverpool, through the Mersey Tunnel, along the motorway and over the familiar route, until at last she turned in at the gates of Wolverley Manor.

She was surprised at the change in the property. She might have been entering any well-ordered farm. Sheep and cattle grazed in the fields and at the rear of the manor in the stableyard a couple of collies sauntered about. They regarded her with idle curiosity. The barns were full of straw and in a sty plump sows grunted contentedly. But through an archway leading to more buildings it was a different story. These buildings had been converted into workspaces for small firms.

Like a neat mews street, five large airy units looked out on to the cobbled yard and nameplates guided visitors to the different individual craftsmen—a leatherworker, a potter, an artist specialising in local scenes, a girl whose wares were embroidered and patchwork articles of every kind, and an antique shop.

Jenni parked the van and in a bemused state wandered into the first of these small shops—the pottery. On the drive down she had had to concentrate on the busy traffic flow and now that she was actually here, within minutes of seeing Clay, she needed time to gather her thoughts, to assemble words with which to open the confrontation.

'Some rich fellow from the south end of the Wirral bought the farmland.' The potter was in a conversational mood. 'He's having a modern place built for himself and he had these old buildings done up and let them to us. But the old house has been standing empty ever since the contents were sold. The agents couldn't seem to get a buyer. But there's a chap been pottering around here the last few days. Looks as if he might be the one. We've only been here a couple of weeks, but it's a lovely place to work and already we're doing a good trade.'

Jenni moved next to the antique shop. The premises were as large as any small conventional shop and there was plenty to look at. But today the crammed shelves could not hold her interest. She had just reached a point where she had nerved herself to go up to the house and seek Clay out, when, 'Jenni?'

And then the shop revolved around Jenni and dissolved, as she saw Clay standing in the doorway.

When she came to her senses she was lying on a camp-bed in a room she had never seen before. Wonderingly, she stared around her. The room was unfurnished, apart from the bed. But before she had time to take in any more than that, Clay entered carrying a glass.

'It's only water, I'm afraid,' he said stiffly

as he proffered it. 'There's nothing else in the house.'

He moved away and stood at the foot of the bed regarding her, his expression unfathomable.

'I didn't think you were the fainting kind,' he observed.

'I'm not,' Jenni said. 'But . . . but I haven't had anything to eat today,' she realised. 'And seeing you . . .'

'You mean you didn't know you'd find me here?' he enquired ironically.

'Yes . . . at least I hoped . . .'

'It seems you've made a new life for yourself. New boyfriend, an engagement ring. Why have you come here, Jenni?' He ground out the words. 'To torment me?'

'I'm not engaged,' she said quickly, holding out her bare left hand as proof. 'I don't have a boyfriend. Tim is Sonia's fiancé. That day you saw us together—in Ormskirk—we were checking the size of the ring.'

Clay was obviously taken aback. Varied emotions chased themselves across his face but it was impossible to tell which was uppermost.

'I had to see you,' Jenni went on, 'to explain . . .'

'Why should you think I'd be interested? Things between us were already over.'

'Then why did you say you'd given in to an impulse to see me just once more?' Jenni demanded. But he didn't answer. 'I was hoping by now you'd have cooled off, realised that I was only repeating what Melinda said because you insisted. Clay,' she said when he still made no answer, 'I *love* you. I know you're not the kind of man Melinda tried to make out. I never believed for one moment the awful things she said about your sisters, and now that I've met them . . .'

'You've met them?' He advanced upon her now, towering threateningly over her where she still sat on the bed. 'Where? How? What have you said to them? If you've . . .'

'Clay!' She wriggled off the bed and stood up. He was so close that she could feel the warmth emanating from his body and it was hard to think clearly and rationally. 'If you'd just listen for a moment, I'll explain.'

'It had better be good,' he told her grimly.

'I went to see Nobby and Deborah. I begged them to tell me where to find you.'

'You must have put up a pretty good show to get past Deborah,' Clay commented, but Jenni couldn't tell whether he was being sarcastic or not.

'She took me to see Clare and Georgie. Oh, Clay, they're lovely people.' Her eyes filled with tears. 'And it's so sad about Clare. It must be awful for you, for all of you. And I understand now why you wouldn't tell me about your private life. You're not the kind of man to brag about his good deeds.'

'Good deeds!' Clay exploded. 'You don't think of it in those terms when it's your family that . . .'

'I know! I know!' Jenni interrupted. 'But even so, not many men would have done what you've done—put them before your own happiness, made yourself poor in their interests.'

'Jenni——' His voice was softer now and his eyes had lost their hardness too. 'I don't know what you hope to gain by coming here and telling me all this. It doesn't make any difference, you know.'

'Why not?' she demanded hardily. 'Don't you love me any more?'

'Oh, Jenni.' It was a cry that seemed dredged up from the innermost depths of him. 'Don't torture me like this.'

'*Do* you love me, Clay?' She moved closer to him, put her hand on his arm and felt his rigid control break.

His arms around her, the feel of his strong chest against her cheek were endearingly familiar and Jenni made a strange sound somewhere between a groan and a sob.

'You know I love you, dammit. And I suppose I never really believed you capable of crediting Melinda's foul imaginings. But it was a convenient way of breaking with you.'

'You wanted an excuse to break with me?' That hurt, and Jenni's eyes were drowned with tears once more as she looked up at him.

'Not wanted—needed,' he contradicted. 'If I could have had what I wanted I would have asked you to marry me. Making love to you just wasn't enough any more. I was beginning to want you with me always—under my roof—in my bed. But as I couldn't . . .'

'You said you couldn't afford to get married,' Jenni said slowly. 'But if what Clare and Georgie told me is true, that isn't so now.'

'That was part of it,' Clay admitted. 'But after the disastrous mess my life became when

Clare had to come and live with us, I swore . . .'

'That no one should ever hurt your sisters again,' Jenni finished for him, 'I know, Georgie told me.'

'Georgie seems to have told you an awful lot.' His tone was curious. 'She must have taken to you.'

'I think she did. I think they both did. I hope so. Oh, Clay, you can't believe that I'd ever treat your sisters the way Melinda did?' Suddenly Jenni's courage and her legs gave out and she sat down on the side of the bed again.

Clay sank down beside her, and his proximity sent a torrent of desire rippling through her veins.

'No, I don't think you would. But . . .'

'Then *why*, *oh why*, didn't you tell me about them? We've wasted so much time,' she mourned.

'Because I suppose I knew, with your generous giving nature, that you wouldn't hesitate to take on my family. But what kind of life is it I'd be offering you? It would be bound to put a strain on our marriage. Clare and I are very close. We always will be until . . . until . . .' His voice cracked and impulsively Jenni threw her arms around him.

'I know, I know,' she said as she hugged him. 'But I don't agree with you. It wouldn't be a strain. I'm not Melinda. I could help you look after Clare. I'd like to. I liked *her*.'

'Jenni, my darling,' his voice was ragged. 'If you only knew how I wish . . . But I can't ask that of you. It would be . . .'

'You're not asking,' she said fiercely, 'I'm offering. Clay, I'm begging you to let me.'

She dared a swift glance at him and found his blue eyes burning with a strange feverish fire. Strangely, he changed the subject.

'I'm buying Wolverley Manor.'

'I gathered that.'

'I was as attracted by it as you were. I felt I'd like to try and put into effect the plans that we talked about. I was going to make it into a new home. I couldn't go back to the Beeches even though Melinda will have to leave.'

He stood up and began to pace the room and with his gaze no longer upon her she could feast her eyes on him, on every remembered line and sinew.

'It wouldn't have been the same without you, but I was going to make it into a new home for myself and the girls. Though Georgie will marry some day, I suppose, and Clare . . .' again that break in his voice, 'Clare won't be with me always.'

'And then you'd be alone—and lonely,' Jenni said. 'Clay, won't you at least give me a chance to prove what I say?'

'And if it doesn't work out?' he said bitterly. 'What then? Am I to be left with more broken pieces of my life to put together?'

'It *will* work.' Jenni broke off. 'You know,' she said in sudden amazement at herself, 'I've never done anything like this before—pestered a man to marry me!'

Clay laughed suddenly, a laugh that was almost a sob.

'I'd forgotten this power you have of amusing me—of lightening my black moods. Oh, Jenni,' he made a helpless gesture that accorded oddly with his powerful build, his inherent masculinity, 'I *have* missed you.'

'And I've missed you.' She waited, watching his face, watching his struggle with himself. He was standing by the window, in profile against the light. She stood up and moved towards him, put a tentative hand on his arm. 'Clay?'

He took both her hands in his and she knew an anguished hunger to be in his arms, closer to him, part of him.

'You still love me, Jenni?' he said wonderingly. 'You still want me?'

'Yes! Oh, Clay, yes.'

His grasp of her hands increased and he pulled her closer, bending his head towards her. His kiss was hard, dominating, compelling. She could feel the vibrations of his body, smell the familiar warm scent of him. She had dreamed about this moment often enough, waking in the mornings to the cold knowledge of reality. As he crushed her to the full length of his long hard body, sexual excitement cascaded through her. His hand brushed her breast. At once her nipple hardened to his touch and she knew the fact had not escaped him, for he drew in an unsteady breath.

His kiss gentled and, as his tongue began a slow sensuous exploration of her mouth, her arms slid around his neck and her response ignited him to greater passion, the increased hardness of his body revealing that his need was as great as her own.

Her blouse had parted from the waistband of her skirt and his hands were moving over her bare skin, stroking her breasts, catching the nipples between his fingers, stirring her to exquisite pleasure. But then his hands sought further intimacies as he murmured a plea against the delicate shell of her ear. Gently but firmly she pushed his questing hands away.

'No, Clay! Not unless you're prepared to marry me. This time it's all or nothing.'

'Yes—I'll marry you—if you'll have me.' His voice was almost humble.

'You know I will. Oh, Clay!' There was a wealth of tenderness in her tone. 'And it will work out, I promise you.'

'Jenni! My darling Jenni. When will you marry me? Soon? I don't think I could bear to wait too long.'

'Yes. Soon. Very soon.' Strange that she should feel so ridiculously shy, after all they had been to each other in the past. But then she turned her lips into the strong column of his neck and at the feel of his warm flesh desire surged anew. 'But you . . . you don't have to wait,' she murmured.

She felt the muscles of his neck convulse and for a moment she thought it was with strong emotion. Then he held her away so that he could look into her face. He was smiling. But then, 'Now?' he asked as if afraid to believe it.

'Now!' she agreed ardently, and with that his control broke.

'Oh, dear lord,' he groaned as he pulled her down with him on to the bed. 'I love you. I love you.'

Their hands trembled as they undressed each other. His heart was pounding so much that she could hear it, his body taut with the need that drove them both.

Clay made love to her as if nothing else in the world had any existence and she caressed his smooth bronzed flesh, meeting his demand with her own, bringing gasps of agonised pleasure from him. In the many times they had made love it had never been quite like this, the relief of starving senses.

For a while they slept and when Jenni woke it was to find herself still held securely in Clay's arms as if he feared even now she might vanish. She kissed his cheek. His eyes flickered open.

'It's true,' he murmured, 'you *are* here.' He smiled a long lazy smile of pure happiness. 'Fate has been good to us after all, my love, hasn't she?'

'Very,' she agreed. 'Oh, Clay, it seemed so long since we'd made love. I couldn't wait. You must think me utterly shameless.'

'Oh, utterly,' he agreed. And then, as she threatened him with a playful fist, 'No, you are adorable and very courageous.' He sat up and looked down at her soberly. 'For it must have taken a lot of courage to come here and face me the way you did.'

'I was scared,' she admitted, 'oh, not of you, but of the way you might react. I don't know what I would have done if you'd sent me away.'

'I might have sent you away,' he said, 'if you hadn't been so persistent. But somehow I don't think we would have been apart for long. Even if we'd been too stiff-necked, I think Fate would have found a way to bring us together again and,' humorously, 'I've never believed in fighting Fate.'

They lay in contented silence for a moment, held

close in each other's arms. Slowly at first, then with more intensity they began to kiss again. Then against Clay's mouth Jenni chuckled softly.

'What now?' he demanded, a smile already spreading across his face.

'Do you know what I think is fated to happen now?' she asked demurely.

'I think I can guess, but I'd rather you told me.'

Snuggled even closer to his hardening body, her own responding even as she spoke, Jenni told him.

## Coming soon
## to an easy chair near you.

**FIRST CLASS** is Harlequin's armchair travel plan for the incurably romantic. You'll visit a different dreamy destination every month from January through December without ever packing a bag. No jet lag, no expensive air fares and *no* lost luggage. Just First Class Harlequin Romance reading, featuring exotic settings from Tasmania to Thailand, from Egypt to Australia, and more.

**FIRST CLASS** romantic excursions guaranteed! Start your world tour in January. Look for the special **FIRST CLASS** destination on selected Harlequin Romance titles—there's a new one every month.

NEXT DESTINATION:
**AUSTRALIA**

  *Harlequin Books*

JTR3

# Take 4 bestselling love stories FREE

## Plus get a FREE surprise gift!

## Special Limited-time Offer

### Harlequin Reader Service®

Mail to

| In the U.S. | In Canada |
|---|---|
| 3010 Walden Avenue | P.O. Box 609 |
| P.O. Box 1867 | Fort Erie, Ontario |
| Buffalo, N.Y. 14269-1867 | L2A 5X3 |

**YES!** Please send me 4 free Harlequin Presents® novels and my free surprise gift. Then send me 6 brand-new novels every month, which I will receive months before they appear in bookstores. Bill me at the low price of $2.24* each—a savings of 26¢ apiece off cover prices. There are no shipping, handling or other hidden costs. I understand that accepting the books and gift places me under no obligation ever to buy any books. I can always return a shipment and cancel at any time. Even if I never buy another book from Harlequin, the 4 free books and the surprise gift are mine to keep forever.

*Offer slightly different in Canada—$2.24 per book plus 69¢ per shipment for delivery. Sales tax applicable in N.Y. Canadian residents add applicable federal and provincial sales tax.

106 BPA CAP7 (US)                                                                       306 BPA U105 (CAN)

Name _____ (PLEASE PRINT)

Address _____ Apt. No. _____

City _____ State/Prov. _____ Zip/Postal Code _____

This offer is limited to one order per household and not valid to present Harlequin Presents® subscribers. Terms and prices are subject to change.

PRES-BPADR                                                        © 1990 Harlequin Enterprises Limited

They went in through the terrace door. The house was dark, most of the servants were down at the circus, and only Nelbert's hired security guards were in sight. It was child's play for Blackheart to move past them, the work of two seconds to go through the solid lock on the terrace door. And then they were creeping through the darkened house, up the long curving stairs, Ferris fully as noiseless as the more experienced Blackheart.

They stopped on the second floor landing. "What if they have guns?" Ferris mouthed silently.

Blackheart shrugged. "Then duck."

"How reassuring," she responded. Footsteps directly above them signaled that the thieves were on the move, and so should they be.

*For more romance, suspense and adventure, read Harlequin Intrigue. Two exciting titles each month, available wherever Harlequin Books are sold.*

INTA-1

# Harlequin Presents®

## Coming Next Month

Available in March wherever paperback books are sold, or through Harlequin Reader Service:

In the U.S.
P.O. Box 1397
Buffalo, N.Y.
14240-1397

In Canada
P.O. Box 603
Fort Erie, Ontario
L2A 5X3